Married to the

Pen

By

Flenardo

Copyright © 2016 by Flenardo

Publisher's Note: This is a work of fiction. Names, characters, places and incidents are product of the author's imagination. Locale and public names are sometimes used for atmospheric purposes. Any resemblance to actual people, living or dead, or to businesses, companies, events, or institutions are completely coincidental.

Published and Edited by

    Creolistic Ink Publishing

ISBN:

    ISBN 13: 978-0692628928
    ISBN 10: 0692628924

Designed by:

    BRANDCONCEPTS
    Contact info: (770) 885-6486

CUNNILINGUS CORNER

This book will be a Top Seller; it is Brilliantly written, I was satisfied in more ways than one, it took me places I never thought I would go, I did not want to put it down. Great poetry throughout the book. I loved the awesome characters, this is truly one of the best books I've ever read. It is Erotic/Hot/Raw/Sexy/Wet/ Blunt & Orgasms to the MOON...

Sincerely,
Shelby Welchel

Flenardo has done it again! He has used his strong and sexual appearance through an array of characters with perfect seduction! The infamous Malakai and Asperilla erotic tales are soul-bond between freaks. "*Married to The Pen*," takes you on a roller coaster of sensations, with pleasure leading the way. An action packed tale of erotica that leaves you wanting more.

Sincerely,
Melissa Griffin-Richardson

This book was phenomenal. The perfect blend of love, sex, and action. Even the perfect time of the month to release it. Flenardo has definitely out done himself this time. I love the surprise twist. There's never a dull moment and I stayed engaged. Awesome book!

Sincerely,
Tiya Thomas

Wow Wow Wow!!!! Malakai and Asperilla are at it again! Excitement and Hotness lays in every page turned. This couple brings the heat and a love that is truly all their own. *Married to The Pen* had me glued to my seat not wanting it to end... This Twisted tale of Love, Lust, and Madness does not disappoint your appetite for more! Flenardo you did your thing! You have created a literary style all your own which weaves poetry and an excellent storyline like only you can! A truly Exciting Read!

Sincerely,
Natasha Wright

DEDICATION

This book is dedicated to everyone who believes and encourages me.

To my beautiful wife Charmaine, it's never easy to share me with the world but success wouldn't be complete without your presence.
I love you.

To my Aunt Janette thank you for telling the community.

To my Caribbean/Puerto Rican family. Casmore & Joselyn Lewis. Arlington & Zoey Bergan. Honored to be a part of the family.

Chapter 1

Necole

After two years of boredom, my sister is released from the psychiatric ward today. It is partially my fault she was committed. She's willing to do anything to ensure my happiness which includes helping me fight for a man belonging to another woman. The first time I heard his voice on the CD, I played with my pussy on every track. Juices ran to my asshole as I stood fantasizing how I would fuck the life out of him.

It seemed like yesterday when we drove from California to Florida for his performance. I wasn't too keen on Nikki's idea at first but it turned out to be an adventurous one.

Everything was perfect until we ran out of gas near a truck stop filled with lonely men. Some women have the gift of gab but I have the gift of slab. I can stuff more dicks in my mouth than a Thanksgiving turkey. Back in high school I slurped off the football team and coined Ms. Slobber Knocker.

Enough of my naughty past; I know you all are dying to hear what happened at the truck stop.

Where did I leave off? Oh yeah.

The car died on the side of the road to Tampa because we forgot gas at the last exit.

"Bitch, you thinking about Malakai running his dick in your ass. You forgot to check the gas hand," Nikki shouted.

"Fuck you hoe! Your trifling ass blasting his CD knowing I can't function with his voice in my ears. You didn't drive through Texas. Sit back and figure out a way to get some gas." I yelled.

"Yeah Yeah Yeah! I didn't drive because you would have masturbated to Louisiana; squirting on the windows and shit. The wipers don't clean the insides." She joked and flipped her middle finger.

"Nikki, you are on some bullshit but there are lights ahead. I'm sure we can find someone to help."

"You find help! I need a dick to cure this itch since we left Arizona."

We argued, exited the car, and walked for what seemed like eternity. We reached the truck stop; a perfect scenery for a nasty bitch like Nikki. The atmosphere filled with smoke and beer belly men wearing cowboy boots.

"Nothing like white meat between your teeth and booty cheeks," Nikki admitted smacking her ass for the truckers.

She climbed into the first truck and within five minutes she came out with a wad of bills.

"Here's your damn gas money! Let's up the ante on tonight competition."

"What the hell are you talking about now?"

"A suck-a-thon. There are twenty-five trucks and the one swallowing the most cock wins Malakai's heart."

"Bitch you stupid! Dick and everything about him belongs to me. Did you forget you fucked my prom date's brother in the bathroom?"

"Girl, that's high school shit. Tonight is all about Malakai; your throat verses his heart. Are you ready to play?"

I pulled my hair in a ponytail and lashed out, "Bitch I'm not the one for drama and you are not fucking my man."

You would have thought I had wings attached to my soul as I jumped in the first truck. He was a slimy looking muthafucka but my throat never swallowed defeat.

"Don't say shit, pull your dick out!"

I swished a good amount of spit and spewed it; jacked his shaft to strengthen and relax his mind.

Before his eyes rolled in his head, my mouth was wide open, slurping, licking his precum and playing with his balls as my head bounced up and down on his lap.

"Cum for me daddy. I'm your naughty hoe. Fuck my tight juicy mouth. Polish my teeth with cum paste."

I felt his inches hitting the back of my throat but he couldn't handle the power of the slobber knocker. I made sure this cowboy remembered I'm a wild stallion refusing to be tamed.

I slowly eased my head up but kept the tip of his dick in my mouth; jacking with hands of fire. My tongue created a powerful back and forth wave across his head. For the first time, this bastard tried talking shit.

"Yeah baby! I'm going to explode in that black mouth," he moaned.

He bounced up and down in his seat, grabbed the door handle for leverage as I sucked out his oxygen. It's funny how guys become bitches before a sexual seizure.

"I'm cumming baby, please don't stop! I love you. I fucking love you." He screamed while shaking.

His cum shot out like a streak of lighting and I was ready to be struck down and electrified. I swallowed all of it and kept slurping when he pushed my head.

"Sorry, I can't handle it when my dick gets sensitive."

I checked my watch and the timing was on schedule. At this rate I can easily knock out fifteen truckers in less than an hour.

"Thanks for letting my throat hitchhike your cock." I collected my money, left a smile on his face and jumped to the next truck.

"Excuse me, Excuse me Ma'am, are you listening? They are calling your name."

Awakened from my daydream and realized I am in the hospital waiting on Nikki.

Damn I guess you all will have to find out who won the contest another time.

Nikki comes from the office and I jump in her arms. I can't believe she faked a mental illness but now we have enough money to take care of business.

I overhear the doctor advising her to contact him without any hesitations if she needs any medical attention or someone to speak with.

"You have done more than enough. I am ready to go home," Nikki says.

She signs the release forms and out the door we go.

"Where is my car?" Nikki asks.

"It's at the car lot with a red bow. I didn't want anyone suspicious."

"Whatever! I guess I can ride the bus one last time."

"You have a makeover at the spa tomorrow."

"Girl who needs a makeover, I woke up like this."
Laughs flipping her hair back.

She sings her favorite song by *Beyoncé*.

> *You wake up, flawless*
> *Post up, flawless*
> *This diamond, flawless*
> *This rock, flawless*
> *My rock, flawless*
> *I woke up like this.*

"Nikki I am glad you kept your sense of humor."

"They can never take that away from me. I acted normal to get released early."

"I love you Necole."

"And I will forever love you Nikki."

Chapter 2

Malakai

It has been a year since Love Divine's death and I can still hear her voice saying, "Malakai stop fucking those hoes."

My dick has been sober for 9 months; I hope you all didn't think I could go cold turkey. I went on a fucking spree; slaughtering pussy like God did the firstborn in Egypt. Knocking down every ethnic group on the planet and performed threesomes a couple of times to complete my mission.

Asperilla will slice my balls if she finds out about my sexual adventures. To stay focus and faithful until our wedding, I enrolled in rehab for sex addicts. This is the third class and honestly, I love the people and their wild lives. Today is the first time to share my story after being pressured by the group leader Shantae Wells.

She is a thick and sexy redbone with a spider tattoo between her breasts. The legs crawl out of her shirt; they should call her Black Widow because I know her pussy squirts venom.

"Malakai! Malakai! Quit thinking about pussy and share your story," she commands.

Snapping out of my dick thoughts, I look around and notice all eyes are on me.

Ahem! Please excuse me. My name is Malakai and I am a member of Orgasmic Rehab. After a few STD's, getting caught up and almost losing my life over pussy, I couldn't stop fucking. I am a firm believer the sunrise meant my dick should rise and I shall fuck again."

"Malakai, when did you realize you were a whore?" She asks.

"It happened the first time my mom took me to church as a child; I threw pennies on the floor and looked under ladies' skirt. Even as a young freak, I had a lot of nasty thoughts inside of me. Before I became a poet, I worked in a supply store and my supervisor was a voluptuous older woman. Damn shame I don't remember her first name but they're all the same after a dick down."

"Amen!" Shouts one of the brothers giving another Hi-five.

The ladies join in with laughter and comments about their many partners.

"Calm down Super Freaks. Please allow Malakai to finish his story. I can use it for my dildo party tonight," Ms. Wells informs.

"Anyway! I used to masturbate in strange places every time I thought of her. One day I released some steam in her supply room by pulling my dick through the zipper and closing my eyes. I was a virgin but had skills with stroking my shit. In my mind I taught her a lesson as she sucked my dick on her knees. I griped it tight; thrusting my ass in the air fucking her throat dry."

"Yeah Bitch! You ain't talking shit now. I bet I'll be employee of the month. Open your cunt mouth wider dammit!"

"Unbuttoned my pants, underwear dropped to the floor, and continued pleasuring. Right before I came, the damn door opened."

There I was, dick in hand and staring. How the hell do I explain to my parents I am fired for beating my meat at work?

"What the hell? I am calling the police on you for indecent exposure." She screamed.

"Please don't. I can quit and you don't have to pay me this week."

She looked in my eyes and grabbed my dick.

"You are going to jail if you don't eat my pussy," she ordered tapping between her legs.

I have never eaten pussy but I was willing to do anything to escape this situation.

"Pull your pants up and lock the door."

I thought about running however at 15 years old and scared shitless, I obeyed.

Locked the door and found her naked on top of a box; legs opened and panties twirled in her hand.

My mind bounced from left to right asking what if I didn't eat it right and arrested anyway?

"Put these panties on your head and eat my pussy, dick beater!" She insisted.

I never had a woman speak in that tone; it turned me on as spit ran out of my mouth.

Placed them on my head like a skull cap and dropped to my knees. She spread her lips; I closed my eyes and unleashed my whipped tongue like a dog drinking water.

"What the fuck are you doing?" She screamed.

"Hell I don't know; this is my first time."

"You see this piece of meat right here is a clit and your new home. Now suck it!"

She pointed and grabbed the back of my head. I sucked on it like candy as she moaned and twirled her hips.

"You enjoy sucking your boss pussy, don't you dick beater."

I couldn't say shit with a mouthful of juices and pubic hair. Every time her hips rotated my tongue copied the movements.

"Faster dammit! Faster! Eat this pussy like your life depends on it."

Her juices dribbled to the back of my throat. My dog Rocko would be amazed how I'm eating pussy better than he drinks.

Her hips rocked off the box and legs shook with each slash I gave as her screams echoed.

"Yes! Dick beater, get all this cum and you better not spit it out."

She is fucking crazy and I am praying she lets me go home.

The tempos of moans were deeper as she shouted, "Right there. Ahh! Ahh! Ahh! I'm bout to. I'm bout to."

I anticipated her last word to come when I felt a sensational fruit gusher tidal wave in my mouth. Her juices exploded and I loved the taste.

I pulled my head from her slushy lips after the jerking stopped.

She opened her eyes, looked down and said, "Good boy, well done for your first time."

"Are you calling the police?" I asked.

"Baby the only thing I am calling is your black ass three times a week. Next lesson is fucking."

She dressed, kissed my lips and said, "You are getting promoted."

"That's the end of my story for ya'll horny bastards!"

Some of the group members have "let's fuck after class" eyes. I usually get them after a few erotic poems but this is on another level.

"Well class, the discussion is over for today and you all can thank Malakai for the wonderful tale of getting some tail," Ms. Wells says.

The class laughs and exchange hugs before leaving.

I open my car door when someone calls my name, "Malakai wait up!"

Shit! It's the blonde with the nice tits.

"Koley right?" I ask.

"Yes you remember. I thought being a celebrity you would pass up average ladies."

"Well, you don't know anything about me. I am as humble as they come. How can I help you?"

"My pussy is throbbing and I want to fuck thinking about your story."

"Listen Koley, I rarely spare women but I turned over a new leaf. You should have caught me at the beginning of the year and I would have given you the muffle butter special."

"Malakai, I think the term is truffle butter and you can serve it any way you like."

"Nah the term is muffle butter, meaning I'll fuck you in the ass and stick my dick in your mouth."

"Damn! I'm speechless." She says.

"Koley, I mistreated a lot of women in the past and I'm not adding your name. Do you even know what your pussy is worth? Let's be friends and nothing else."

"My friends said you were arrogant and they were right."

"Excuse me; Fuck you and your friends! Take your ass in the building and ask Ms. Well for extra credit or something. I have pleasured you enough."

I start the car and she screams kicking the door, "You ain't shit."

I recently bought my *McLaren* and this dick muncher dent it. I look in my rearview mirror and it is about to get worse.

I roll down the window, "Koley, now is the perfect time to run."

She creates a scene and shouts, "Fuck you."

I thought my evening would be drama free, but here it comes.

BOOM!!!

Flenardo

Chapter 3

Asperilla

Aww how cute, Malakai is staying faithful by hanging out with sex addicts. Maybe he is serious about the engagement and burying his cheating ways. I pray it helps but I'm going to recruit a bitch or two and make more money. I should have thought of this sooner; women fucking for free and going to class telling fuck stories. They can dress as naughty school girls and fulfill my college tour Malakai shut down.

Here comes my man now. He has no idea I parked a couple of cars behind him. I've been on my best behavior since the First Lady's death but my new life is boring as fuck. I have been faithful and my bisexual side shouldn't count. Lucky for him I haven't allowed another woman to sneeze on my clit; well not yet.

Let me get the hell out of here because for once Malakai is doing something right. I am ready to leave when a white woman stops him.

Damn that bitch has some beautiful titties!

I guess I'll wait and see what's about to happen. I slide my window down and open my ears toward their direction.

I can't understand the entire conversation but very impressive how Malakai walks away. He is turning down pussy. Oh My!

I guess I will trust him about ten percent.

The outside shouting snaps me out of my sexual fantasy and finally, I can see action.

A new white bitch will appear on *WorldStar* in a minute. She's throwing a temper tantrum and he's probably belittling her image with a few words.

Okay, I have seen enough. He won't hit her but I will.

He hears the sound of my stilettos clacking across the pavement. As soon as I approach the car, he turns around.

"What the hell are you doing here?" Malakai asks.

"You are always saving me and I'm here to return the favor. Call me Asperilla the Avenger."

"Please don't start any shit Asperilla, I'm going home."

"Too late Rehab Boy."

"Hey Blondie! Get your ass off my car before I drag your face across this parking lot."

Her attention switches to me and asks, "Who the fuck are you?"

"I'm your God. Apologize to my car, my man and take your ass home before you wake up in the hospital."

"Bitch, I ain't doing shit!"

She places her arms across her chest and continues talking. I slip off my 6-inch stiletto and bury the heel cap in her mouth. I try to knock out a tooth but settle for a bloody lip.

"Blondie, I told your dumbass to go home but you're hardheaded."

I blow on my engagement ring and bash her face. "Apologize to the car hoe!"

She cries as I drag her to the door, pressing her face against it, she kisses the dent and apologizes.

It doesn't take long for someone to call the police.

"You know you are going to jail," Malakai reveals.

"Yeah I know but I needed the action. Call Jaz or Cherry to bring my Jag home."

I grab Blondie's purse and get her ID, "Koley Regean, 705 East Jackson Street. Listen Blondie; if you say anything, you will never see daylight. Do you understand me?"

"Yes."

I slap her again, apply my lip gloss and wait for the police.

"You are a damn fool," Malakai says.

"Maybe, but this legit living is for the birds. I liked your ass more when you were whoring."

"I can make that happen if you like."

"Just because I like it don't mean you can."

Before he thinks of something slick to say. I pull my blade out of my hair and run it across his face. "Do it and lose your dick."

"There you go threatening to cut off what you love." He laughs and says, "I'll see you at home."

"Yes you will but not too early, I have a surprise."

Tampa's finest interrupts our conversation.

Usually the police ask a million questions but a bloody bitch on the ground and fingers pointing in my direction, I guess I'm off to see the captain.

"Asperilla Valdez, not you again," the officer states.

"Yes in the flesh," I respond doing my signature Dorothy heel clap.

The crowd laugh as the police read my rights. I am handcuffed and placed in the back of the car.

I look and notice Malakai talking to another officer. Knowing his retarded ass, he is telling him to leave me in jail. It doesn't matter because I have a special treat.

The officer comes to the car, starts the ignition and we leave.

"Officer Pernell, take me home and I won't press charges."

"Asperilla, you are out of your mind. You are the one who started everything and it's on video."

"That might be true but she dented my ride. It was only fair to file an ass whooping claim. Where do I get my refund for my nails?"

The officers chuckle and say, "Malakai has taken care of everything."

"The money I post will come back to me after your captain's retirement party next month."

"Yes and we can't wait. Girls were swinging from rafters at the last one."

They finish their conversation as I fade into my thoughts. Beating Blondie's ass was exciting. I haven't had fun in a long time. I'm going to miss this business when Malakai finish his transactions and money laundering.

The car pulls to the station and we go through the rear heading toward the elevators. Guess I am seeing the pussy whipped man in charge.

I enter his office and calmly ask, "Captain how much is bail?"

"Asperilla no need. Will Jaz be there?"

"Yes Captain Ramos, your favorite woman will be there. You might want to slow down because your blue pill doesn't stop heart attacks."

He laughs and says, "You might be right but I don't plan on living forever plus the party is sponsored by my late wife's insurance."

I wouldn't give a damn if it was *Michelle Obama*'s money; I want to see it tossed up.

Then *Nicki Minaj* chorus pops in my head.

Ass fat, yea I know
You just got cash, blow some mo'
Blow some mo', blow some mo'

"Asperilla are you paying attention to me?"

"Excuse me Captain Ramos; I was counting money in my head. No need to worry, everything will be perfect for your last ride."

"By the way there is no need to post bail. Everything has been taken care of."

We exchange handshakes. he opens the office door and Officer Pernell leads me out the building.

One thing about that jackass man of mine, his operation is impeccable because Cherry and Jaz are here.

"We dropped your car off."

"Thanks ladies."

"You know we have less than a month to plan the retirement party."

"The girls are waiting on the word," Cherry says.

"Wonderful! Malakai is flipping business so fast until we might be relaxing in a foreign country soon."

"*Dubai*," Jaz shouts.

"Your ass watched *Furious 7* too much but I agree we have enough pussy power to make *Sheikh Mohammed* empty his account."

"I'm down for a flight," Cherry says cranking the car.

"It does sound irresistible. I'll see what I can plan under Malakai's nose," I admit.

The conversation is pleasant and this past year has been great between me and the ladies. We have truly become sisters. I miss Ayanna but she left and Malakai reinstated my rein.

As the car arrives to the gate I give the code to Cherry for entry.

"Your house is beautiful," Jaz speaks in amazement.

"Thank you."

We pull to the front, I exit and tell them to expect a call next week.

On Fridays Malakai heads to the club before coming home and that's exactly what I need to fulfil a crazy fantasy. If he is staying faithful, then I am creating every diabolical sex scene to keep his dick jumping 24-7.

Chapter 4

Malakai

It's a blessing having the police on your payroll and their tongue in your girls' hole. The incident with Asperilla was not my fault; I tried to warn Koley to run; mama always said a hard head makes a soft ass. I hope Ms. Wells lets me back in class next week.

After watching Officer Pernell take her downtown, I meet with some investors and watched the Spaced Age Freak show. Tonight is going to be one of the nastiest erotic performances in Florida. I appreciate how everyone supported the name rebirth from Poetic Heaven to Love Divine at the grand opening.

We are the most talked about spot in the city that caters to every ethnic group every other night.

I speak to a few members before heading to my office with a one-way mirror watching the entire club. Sometimes I'll focus on a woman as she dances; beat my dick and try to nut before the song is over.

This must be my lucky night seeing a Latino chick with long, jet black hair, tiny waistline and heels.

"Damn Mamacita, can get it!"

Loud knock interrupts my thoughts.

"Who is it?"

"Malakai, it's Monique."

"Come in."

"We have an issue. Mr. Bionic won't be able to perform. his son was rushed to the hospital earlier with a concussion."

"Wow I was bragging the other day on his football skills. Please deliver flowers to the hospital tomorrow. Did we find another poet?"

"No we didn't. That's why I am here. They will get slaughtered without a third guy."

"Fuck it; I'll do it, no need for my introduction."

"The show starts in 10 minutes."

"All I need is 5."

She gives a smile and expresses, "I'll get the music ready."

I look out the window and lost sight of her. She will come to me before the night is over.

I have nothing to wear. I'll go *Tom Cruise* on their asses; gotta love the 80's besides *Risky Business* was one of my favorite movies.

I turn on my speakers and the host announces the first female.

Shit! I'm going to be late.

I strip out of my clothes, grab my *Dalton Cordovan* boots, dress shirt and tie. Run downstairs and stand in the midst of the insane crowd as the last guy is introduced.

I have no idea which song Monique picked but I'm about to make someone a believer.

R. Kelly comes on *"It Seems like You're Ready"* that's my shit!

I grab the first woman from behind, spin her around to see my face and carry her to the middle of the dance floor as she whines.

It is a good thing I'm in artistic mode because I can relapse and fuck the air out of her lungs.

I am beyond ready to advertise as she takes off my shirt. It doesn't take long for a few ladies to flood the floor with panties of every color of the rainbow. Fuck making it rain; rain the scent on me and I'll sniff them later.

The crowd scream, "Malakai, I am ready."

I bring her on stage, grab the mic and sit in the chair.

"Malakai, you know how to make an entrance," says one of the poets."

The female poets look crazy as hell at me.

"You all should have thought of the idea," I boast.

One of them flips the bird and shouts, "It is on now."

The host asks, "Who's performing first?"

I reply, "I will! I am getting raped if I don't put her down."

She turns, throws her legs over my shoulder and twerks real slow; the crowd screams for more. Unlike most ladies pulling their dresses down; she let hers rise. Pussy lips all in my face and I love it. I rip her panties off and the crowd blurts, "Oh Shit."

I wipe my tongue on her panties and lay them on the mic.

All the poets shout, "We ain't using that."

I rub her ass, place two fingers to my lips and silence the crowd.

The ambience is set and I'm about to make her pussy wetter by massaging her inner thighs as I skeet words.

My tongue belongs in your Motherland.
Tasting sweetness of honey and juices from God hands.
Biting on your pussy lips like a jazz band
Waiting to hear the sound waves of your moans
escaping your throat.
Thirsty for your knowledge, your wisdom I can swallow.
Flood my face with the creation of the human race.
Dance in my mouth until your orgasm sparks a fire.
Become a nasty beast, no sheets just raw fucking,
Toe sucking, thrusting and bucking.
Fuck my face until it fades away.
Shout, Eat this pussy! Squeeze your muscles on my lips.
Now spin around and choke on this dick,
Wait! You better not taste.
Before you spit, Spit again!
Rub saliva around my head. Now get sloppy and take it
in your mouth.
Slow slurps. Bite the head. Sink your teeth into it.
Aww shit. Suck it!
Slurp this dick one more time.
Wrap your legs around me.
I'm going to fuck every man that has ever been in you,
out of you.
Now beg for me to cum. I can't hear you.
Beg for me to cum! I hear you baby and I'm cumming.
A couple more thrusts as I dig my nails into your ass
cheeks.
Lying you down and wet your chest with my cum.
A little extra juice for your face.
Tonight every hole on your soul is my mission.
When the dick is hardheaded, the tongue always listens.

After the last word, I stroke my index finger across her pussy lips. She shakes and creams and I couldn't resist licking them; damn she tastes like cherries.

She comes back to Earth after the release.

I ask her name.

"Kimberly."

"Nice to meet you Ms. Kimberly. Thanks for being my muse."

"The pleasure is all mine," she says kissing my cheek.

She stumbles off stage as I fan her juices from my thighs toward the female poets.

"You a cheating muthafucka," they exclaim.

I explode with laughter and ask, "Whose next?"

One of them stand, clap her hand and two guys come to the front of the stage.

She tosses the mics in their direction to hold on their pants like dicks. All of the females leave their seats and perform poetry while demonstrating fellatio.

The crowd scream, "Suck it."

I look at the fellas and admit, "We may be in trouble."

The third female stands behind the second guy, creates a sandwich and spits poetry in his ass. This show is out of hand but nasty and anything unusual can happen.

After the performance, the ladies escort them to their seats. The crowd settles down and the fellas perform.

The men are in raw form. Taking their clothes off and spraying whipped cream on their chest; eight ladies run to the stage to lick. Lean their head back in unison like getting their dicks suck. One of them grabs the female head and spit nasty lyrics.

I am on stage and for that one moment I forget I am engaged. I turn around, snatch my underwear off and wrap it around my dick. I stroke slow in front of the crowd.

The DJ sees me losing it so he plays *"Throw that Dick"* by *2 Live Crew*. The fellas stop performing and the crowd goes ballistic. I lock eyes on the Latino chick from earlier in a tight purple dress and motion to come my way.

I drop to my knees and whack off by her ear. She licks her tongue that's says she wants to be sprayed. I can only think of all the pussy I can't fuck.

Grab my dick with two hands as her mouth opens. Sweat pouring from my forehead; resembling a grenade barrel by the way I am cocking it back and forth.

Damn her mouth looks delicious. Fuck It!

I unleash cum and spray a milky mustache above her lips and soak her dress.

I apologetically say, "I'm so sorry for nutting on you."

She responds, "This dress will be worth a lot of money in a few weeks; Malakai seed for sale. I plan on auctioning it out and make it work for me."

Monique comes on stage with a towel for her and interrupts, "Asperilla is going to kill you when you get home."

"Damn I hadn't performed in a long time, I lost it, at least I didn't fuck her fine ass; shit another story for rehab. Monique if you don't see me in a few days, I am dead."

"You are a retard but I'll visit your gravesite."

Run back to my office, look out the window and the crowd is getting it in. I guess this shit will be on *WorldStar* and *YouTube* tomorrow.

I have done some wild things but never beaten my dick in front of a club. What the hell was I thinking? Being faithful is fucking up my brain cells. I better get it together before I end up in a body bag.

Chapter 5

Asperilla

"Damn who the hell is calling now?"

"Hello!"

"Asperilla, it's me."

"Jaz what the hell do you want at three o'clock in the morning. If you aren't in the bed than your ass need to be giving head and bringing me my bread. Aww shit! Malakai isn't the only poet in this house. Now back to you, wassup!"

"You might want to flip on *YouTube*."

"If you are about to tell me about Malakai beating his dick at the club, save it. I always have an informant. He has the mind of a genius for business but when transformed into a poet, he is stupid as fuck. I told his dumbass he is going to piss off the wrong chick."

"Asperilla I have a question. How do you make ya'll relationship work?"

"Honestly, I have no idea. We were born for each other; the freaky version of Bonnie and Clyde. He spits, I swallow and our future has never been brighter. Now enough of the sensitive shit. I have to save these emotions for my wedding day."

"And one more thing Jaz."

"Yes."

"You better stop looking at my man's dick and playing patty cake with your pussy."

"I know he's a hoe in rehab but he's my hoe. Now get your crazy ass off my phone," I joke pushing the end button.

Malakai stays in trouble but I'll make sure he understands that my dick belongs in my mouth and not on *YouTube*.

Even though I want to kill that bastard; fulfilling my rape fantasy and a couple of nuts in his mouth is my reward.

Malakai pulls into the driveway while I gaze at the moon drifting within the skies.

He already has an idea that I know. Yes, go ahead and open the door so I can laugh at your ass in 3.2.1.

Boom! Boom! Boom!

He could ring the doorbell but men want to display testosterone.

Muthafucka sounding like Captain Caveman, "Asperillaaaaaaaaaaaaaa! Open the fucking door."

His screams entice the moisture in my pussy. Yes! He'll beat this pussy until his dick crawls out of my back.

I wait until he does it again before I go to the window.

"Malakai, what the hell do you want?"

He walks from the porch and looks up. "Why are my locks changed?"

"If they were yours then you wouldn't be outside."

"Fuck you! Open this damn door."

"Why? Are you turning into the Hulk? I'm going to smash this pussy in your face for talking crazy."

"Bitch! I ain't playing with you."

"Oh we are calling people bitches now. Yo bitch is at home washing *Proactive* off her face. Since you want to act like a dog then your dirty dick ass can sleep outside."

"Sleep outside, you are crazy as hell. You already know I have other places to go."

He starts the car engine and I shoot the back window with my *44 Magnum*.

I know he is angry but it is making me hornier by the second.

"Bitch, you could have shot me."

"That bullet wasn't near you and if I wanted you dead, I wouldn't be going through this. Now come in the house before I put a bullet in your ass for real."

"Unlock the door so I can choke the shit out of you."

"You are choking a lot of things tonight. Your dick should be sore."

"Open the damn door Asperilla."

"I ain't doing shit but this." I toss the rope tied to the bed. "Since you like to make thot dreams come true; your black ass can play *Rapunzel* and scale these walls."

"Asperilla I swear you're going to pay when I get there."

"My payment is a hard dick, stiff tongue and your face. Now hurry the fuck up!"

I'm getting angry dick in a few minutes. I was born to spice up a sex life maybe I should write articles for fake ass magazines.

Pick up the remote to the entertainment system and play *Take It* by *Marsha Ambrosia*.

I hear him crawling up the wall as I close my eyes, play in my pussy and moans, "Take It, Take It, Take It, Take It."

I gently stroke my clit to the beat and feel his hands around my neck. He has the perfect grip to enhance an orgasm from out of this world. His teeth sink into my shoulder blades as I take my free hand and stick two fingers in my ass. Feeling his hand easing from my neck and expose my mouth with excitement. I refuse to open my eyes as his dick slaps my face.

"Bitch open wider!" He demands.

I am happy to oblige. Leaning my head off the bed. Swishing my hands across my clit as he tries to gag me.

Looks like my rape scene is going downhill. He lifts me from the bed and hangs upside down against the wall.

"Got Damn You!" I shout.

His tongue enters my lips with no mercy while I deep throat. He nibbles the tip of my clit, chews on my hood and dances his balls on my chin. I have never felt pain so fucking good.

He can get sucked later. I need this nut. Pull his dick out of my mouth and gives the sloppiest hand job as he feasts.

"Eat, you filthy muthafucka! Suck out my fucking ovaries! Ahh shit, show me how much you want it."

He flips around and hangs me out the window with legs wrap around his neck. I better cum before he drops me. Clutching the rope tightly and the only thing I'm letting go is this juicy nut.

I am on the verge of an orgasm when he crams 3 fingers in my asshole; tongue biting and sucking my clit.

"Dig Deeper Malakai. Dig Deeper! Yes! I love you. I'll kill for you. Right There! Right There!"

I thrust my hips as my toes pop, "Oh Shit. Baby. Baby. I'm, I'm, I'm, I'm..." Screaming at the top of my lungs like a newborn baby.

He smiles, pulls me out the window and into the bed. He kisses me and finally says what I want to hear. "I love you Asperilla."

Before I respond, he turns me on my stomach and runs his dick in.

"Bitch you getting this dick tonight!"

When he's in beast mode, I bite on the pillow and take my punishment. His strokes hit all angles and corners.

"Bounce that ass."

I jiggle and bounce the left cheek and then right. I am turning him on even more but damn he is stinging my ass. He presses on my lower back and my body sinks into the bed.

"Hold still! I'm getting this nut."

I release the pillow since he won't cum unless I scream. "Oh Shit. Yes! Beat your pussy."

He yanks my hair, pushes my legs together, cocks his dick back and thrust hard and deep.

"This is for my car. This is for making me climb through the window," he grunts.

"Yes! Slay this pussy," I scream.

We swap tongues and refuse to stop until he cums. I feel our breath escaping from one body to another.

After the last couple of strokes, he releases and everything becomes silent. He pulls away and stares into my eyes twisting my hair.

"Damn you are so fucking beautiful."

His dick goes from Hulk to Bruce Banner and the passion of his inches decreasing causes my pussy to drip.

"Malakai, I truly love you but you have to stop wilding out on stage. Your erotic poetry is mesmerizing. You can spit and not take your dick out for those thirsty hoes. I never have been the jealous type and never will be. I want to spend the rest of my life with you and only you. I met you as a Poet and together we built our empire. It's time to move on to the next chapter. I almost lost you once due to my craziness and I'll be damn if I lose you again. These ladies will kill for dick especially yours. I need us to grow old together until our orgasms squirt dust."

"Asperilla, your ass is stupid."

We laugh holding each other and wait on the sun to rise.

Chapter 6

Nikki

You have no idea how wonderful it is to have your own place. No doctors, no meds, and don't get me started about the nasty food. My new *Mercedes* sits outside and I love our apartment; not as big as I want but pretty soon Malakai will buy one. Today is perfect for riding the pool boy's dick while sipping on a margarita.

"Nikki I have something to show you," Necole says.

Damn, there goes my fantasy. Leave it up to her to mess up my wet thoughts.

"Necole I have only been out a week. Can a bitch have some time to herself?"

"You had two years away from me. It's time to get my baby daddy."

"Your ass ain't pregnant. What the fuck are you talking about?"

"I will be the first time we fuck. I have been praying and claiming it in Jesus name."

She should have said in my name because I am the one that makes her dreams come true. Fuck *50 Cent*, it's Get Malakai or Die Trying.

"Necole tell me what's up."

"Girl you are not going to believe what I saw on *YouTube*."

"Dez Nuts, got em!"

"Quit playing Nikki, this is serious."

"Alright, calm down Necole but that shit was funny as hell. Okay show me."

She spins the computer around and my eyes say damn before my mouth speaks. The way he jacked that dick on stage as if he defied the law of physics. His hand moved faster than the speed of light and my pussy quivered. This is the reason I'll get Malakai for her but she will be sharing.

A lucky Latino woman is blessed with all of that delicious cum. I press my face as close as I could to the screen, open my mouth and envision receiving his scrumptious load.

She snatches it and says, "This is the reason your crazy ass was locked up."

"Nah bitch, it was because of your dead husband. Now who is this bitch about to get a facial?" I ask.

"Her name is Joselyn and she lives in *Carrollwood*."

She flips to another screen and shows the dress auctioning on *Facebook*.

"What! Someone is going to buy a dress with cum stains on it," I shout in disbelief.

"Nikki, we have to get it before it's sold."

"And you call me the crazy one."

"Necole let me do some research and figure out our next move."

"Okay Sis," she says giving a hug and walking away.

My sister is a real life groupie with nothing but Malakai pictures and albums in her room. I don't give a damn about his poetry; I want his money and lifestyle. We were so close at the last show when he ran the mic down her chest.

I knew he would fuck her but he kept talking shit about not fucking fans. What kind of man will tease a woman to death and not bring her to life with dick?

Hell we went all out to impress him. Money was not our best friend back then when I stole a few dresses from *Dillard's* and sucked the sales associate off for shoes. I believe if we could have gotten him alone, Necole would have given the slobber knocker and I would have taken his money and jewelry. It was a soundproof plan but never had the opportunity because of one bitch.

When Necole was talking to him, she walked up and kissed him. She had the nerve to autograph her name on the CD instead of Malakai.

I was pissed and amazed how a bitch had that much swag. I looked at Necole and told her she will pay. Five years later, we are in a better place and its time we cash in on our upgrade.

I walk inside when my phone rings.

"Hello."

"A sister gets out the ward and you can't call a brother," he says.

I knew I should have changed my number, this muthafucka is a nuisance.

"Charles, it's nice to hear from you too."

"Don't play games Nikki. Where the fuck is my money?"

"Watch your tone and you'll get it soon."

"I know you are holding out. I want my half or I'm going to the police."

"You are greedy as hell; that wasn't the agreement."

"Fuck the agreement. Half and nothing less!" He says hanging up the phone.

I can't believe this bastard cut me off. It's not like he had anything hard to do. It was a simple carjacking and he couldn't pull the trigger so I did it. I told him to hide the gun and I will make sure he is paid when the insurance claim was approved. Now he is trying to double cross me. Let me get my ass back in the house and tell Necole about this foolishness.

"Necole," I shout walking in the door.

"Yes. I am in the kitchen."

"Charles called, can you believe this shit?"

"I guess he is looking for the money. What are you going to do?"

"I shouldn't give his cowardly ass shit but he is threatening me with the police."

"Nikki I can't go to jail; my ass is too prissy. They may have me with Big Belinda. Hell naw!"

"No one is going to jail. We will pay Charles a visit. The insurance settlement was only $300,000. It's a good thing you didn't sign a prenup or all the work would have been for nothing. Your ex-husband was an asshole and he deserved to die. I didn't like the way he treated you and even though you married him for the money, no woman deserves to be beaten."

"Who are you telling? I am still shaken up."

"Well we are together and nothing will keep us apart.

"Just like Celie and Nettie," she jokes.

We clap our hands and act our scene from the *Color Purple*. *"Me and you, us never part. Makidada. Me and you, us have one heart. Makidada. Ain't no ocean, ain't no sea. Makidada. Keep my sister away from me."*

"Charles is holding the gun as leverage. We need it before he gets a dime from us."

"I have an idea how to get it."

"Look at my little sister thinking of a master plan. Well I am all ears."

"You know Charles always wanted me, let's give him a taste."

"Being away has drained that memory. He is all yours, I'm out of this one."

"Now back to us. Is there anything you would like to do tonight?"

"I have been dying to go to *Donatello's*, a nice Italian restaurant featuring live jazz."

"It sounds like a wonderful place. I hadn't taken my *Mercedes* anywhere besides the grocery store and the mall. Will there be any guys there?"

"Only Tampa finest," she replies.

"Great, I would love to get drunk and fuck; it has been two years and I need someone between my legs."

"I'm surprised you didn't sweet talk the doctor to fill your prescription."

"Hell, don't think I wasn't tempted. I behaved for your sake. I couldn't leave you."

"What time does it open and do we need a reservation?"

"I believe we can make it online. Give me the phone to check."

"Ok when you find out, let me know I have to run to the bathroom."

I sat on the toilet thirty seconds when Necole plows through the door.

"Tonight times are 7:00, 7:30, and 8:00. Which one?"

"Let's do 8pm. It's enough time to get there without rushing; you know your ass always change into two or more outfits."

"I'll be on time I promise."

"Whatever! Get your ass out so I can get ready."

She walks out the door and I wonder if I have a chance to swallow some Italian sausage tonight. I'm not sure if I am horny or hungry but I will order both.

Chapter 7

Malakai

"I'm always into some shit but it's a blessing I am engaged to a woman who has accepted my whorish ways. Being faithful is not easy but I'm trying because of my promise to you. Last week I was close to having a relapse and wanted to fuck the shit out of a woman at the club. I milked my dick in her face; the cum shot was a work of art and her skin was my canvas. Ahh Shit! Poetry at the grave site. I have to spit these words for you. I will call this piece Tongue Stroke."

"Are you ready? Of Course you are. Ok I'm going in."

Passion to paint words into masterpieces.
My DNA links to Leonardo, Pablo, and Francisco.
No wonder I was birthed the name Malakai.
Created to be different when I write.
Shift people's soul when I recite.
My tongue is able to create brush strokes from never ending paint that runs from my throat.
Everything comes to life, bouncing off the paper.
My imagination becomes invincible and incredible.
Regardless of what the world sees, I am the cage bird Maya set free.
Free to create, inspired to motivate because only normal people walk straight.
I rather take the road less travel, follow the curves.
I am a poet that loves to paint pictures with words.

"So tell me what do you think? I love talking to you. You always have the right thing to say. I'm not perfect but I have come a long way from the last time we were together. Love Divine, I truly miss you."

"Yep you are right. I didn't think of you when I performed at the club. The good news is I'm closer to leaving the business. We have a few jobs to complete, get married, retire, and disappear for a while. Wow the thought of marriage, honestly I wanted to be a whore forever and because of you, I am slowly changing."

If I hadn't been in the game she would be alive. Every day I deal with guilt; her family has forgiven me but I feel responsible for her death.

I can't resist my tears from falling. I believe it's okay for a man to cry. We try to be hard and dominant to hide our emotions. Today I am opening up and releasing this pain.

"Thank you for seeing the good in me. I am a wild man with psychotic ambitions but value your love more. Don't give up on me and please tell God to leave my name on the open mic list."

I place roses on her grave, blow a kiss, and walk to my car. Usually guilt hits me over and over but this time a sign of relief strikes instantly.

Asperilla has a meeting with the ladies tonight about the plans for the retirement party. She is doing an incredible job; it's only a matter of time before something destructive happens.

I leave the cemetery and not sure where I am riding. The sky displays a perfect beautiful view from my red drop top *Camaro*. Fuck it! I'll race the sun and head towards *Pier 60.*

Listening to *All Hands on Deck* by *Tinashe* blast through the speakers as I pull up to the stop light on the main road. Bobbing my head and dancing until I didn't notice the ladies in the car beside me. I tilt my shades, arch my eyebrow like the *Rock* and accelerate when the light turns green.

I reach my destination after driving for 15 minutes and everyone is enjoying their evening. *Sunset Pier 60* is an enchanted spot to do almost anything; movies, live bands, arts & crafts, and of course beautiful women.

I find a decent parking space, change into my summer wear and grab my sandals. Every man should take a little pride in their toes. Never know when your woman might want to dip them in a wine glass.

Let me check out the band and street performers. people are breathing fire, breakdancing, walking on stilts, and men posing as statues. This is definitely a change from the club and the escort life. I can mellow here until I meet Asperilla.

I see the juggler preparing for his set. He pulls out devil sticks and woos the crowd. The little kids are impressed but the older people want more. He juggles a few times and stops as his assistant light the sticks.

Oh shit. I hope this dude don't burn himself.

"Don't worry I'm a professional street performer," he shouts.

He tosses and flips them behind his back. I am excited when his assistant brings a unicycle; he pedals back and forwards.

I act like a little kid at times but fuck that, he is putting in work. He juggles twice, hops off the bike and takes a bow.

The crowd congratulates him with claps and cash. I lay a grand in his hat and turn around. I didn't make it three feet before he shouts out, "Hey. Excuse me Sir."

"You don't have to call me Sir. My name is Malakai."

"It's a habit with the business. I don't want to disrespect someone that supports me."

"I understand. How can I help you?"

"I wanted to thank you for the money. I am good but never made that much in one night. Thank you for blessing us."

"No problem. You are very talented and you deserve it."

We exchange hugs and he runs to his assistant.

The nightlife approaches and I need to get out of *Clearwater* before trouble finds me.

Chapter 8

Nikki

It has been forever since I had some dick so don't be in here acting shy and shit. We are about to run game on these muthafuckas and take their nuts and money. I need you to scope out the room on who's getting fucked. Men do it all the time and it's our turn to leave them feeling shitty.

"Nikki! How many times do I have to tell you that I am saving my pussy for Malakai?"

"Yeah I hear you but tonight you are fucking a stranger and going to love it! Plus, I have an idea to make you see things my way."

"Here you go with these crazy ass ideas."

"Necole, I was in the crazy house, what do you expect?"

Everyone in the restaurant gets quiet like they have never seen two bitches laughing with each other. I wanted to ask what the fuck they are looking at but I made a promise to act civilized.

"What are you ordering?" Necole asks.

I give a cunning grin with a long pause. I know she is waiting for me to say something stupid like meatball with cum sauce. I calmly respond, "I am having the Carpacio Di Fellatio."

"Nikki stop playing. The name is *Carpacio Di Filetto*."

"Girl I know the damn name. My enunciation sounds much wetter."

"Whatever Nikki! Here comes the waiter."

"Yes and he is cute."

"Order for me, I have to run to the restroom."

"Good evening and welcome to *Donatello*. My name is Benito and can I recommend starting your evening with a little champagne?"

"Yes, my sister and I will have a glass of *Moët & Chandon*."

"Excellent choice madam if I must say."

He turns around and I smack his ass. Before he can get out a word I asks, "What time do you get off."

"10pm; don't touch my ass again at least not in public," he says.

I motion for him to come closer as I whisper in his ear, "You are getting fucked by two women tonight. Will that be a problem?"

"No problem at all Ma'am."

"Benito, stop calling me ma'am! My pussy stays juicy and wet."

"Yes Ma."

I press my fingers to his lips and reply, "You like being disobedient, don't you?"

"The manners are my upbringing and I apologize. I don't even know your name."

"My name is Nikki."

"Well Ms. Nikki I have to go before I get in trouble."

"Run along but save your strength. You'll need it later."

I watch his tight ass disappear into the kitchen; in minutes Benito returns with our drinks.

I order our entrees since I have no idea what the hell she is doing in the restroom.

"Benito I will like the *Carpacio Di Filetto*, the *Vitello Dolce Vita*, and the *Salmone Alla Stromboli*."

"That's a lot of food Ms. Nikki. Are you sure you can handle all of that?"

"Baby I can handle more than you can deliver, remember that."

"I'll place this order and get it right to you; enjoy the live music."

"One more thing."

"Yes Ms. Nikki."

"This is my number. Call when you get off."

"I plan on it."

He takes it and head to the kitchen. Where the hell is Necole? Is she taking a shit or something?

She appears and asks, "What did I miss?"

"Everything! What the hell were you doing in there?"

"The line was long if you must know."

"Whatever! Benito is coming over tonight."

"Who the hell is Benito?"

"The cute waiter. If you weren't shitting, you would have met him."

"Fuck you Bitch! I said the line was long."

"Anyway, we will teach him the art of serving and fuck him senseless. I don't want to hear anything about Malakai tonight; let's celebrate and toast balls in our mouths."

"You are stupid as hell Nikki but cheers to your retarded ass."

We drink and listen to jazz until the bottle is empty. I am wondering where the hell is Benito with our order as my stomach growls. I scan the room hoping I didn't get him fired for smacking his ass in front of the owner.

I look down at my watch and count to sixty seconds real slow. I am very impatience and before I get to twenty, the waiter brings our meal to the table.

"You are not Benito, where is he?"

"Please forgive us, it would have been out sooner but Benito had an emergency."

"Well you're not getting his tip. Sit the food down, fetch another bottle of *Moët* and take your merry go lucky ass back into the kitchen."

"Nikki why do you have to be angry all the time," Necole scolds while pounding her fist on the table.

"How about you say grace. Never mind! You are taking too long."

Bless the Lord,
Bless the Cook.
Those that don't have nothing to eat.
Can stand up and look. Amen!

"Why can't we have a nice and quiet evening without drama?"

"Remember I was the one locked up. This is my first taste of freedom maybe I'll act better ummmmmm, never."

I grab Necole's hand and admit, "I am sorry. For the rest of the night I will behave. I'll do it because I love your spoiled ass."

"Excuse me Necole, how is your salmone?"

"My salmon is better than your Italian accent."

I bring a smile to her face and she forgave me for being rude earlier. I love my sister and will kill anyone to fulfill her happiness.

We continue eating when the music touches my soul.

"I'll be right back Necole."

"Where the hell are you going?"

"Relax! I'm going to the bar and ask one of the guys to dance."

"Go ahead Nikki but be careful."

Walk to the bar and extend my hand to a gorgeous white man with dazzling blue eyes, dark hair, and fitted suit.

Damn, he is the total package. He has to be a CEO, short for Coochie Eating Octopus. He better has the type of tongue that emulates eight tentacles.

"My name is Corbin," he says kissing my hand.

His lips melt my skin and tongue rolls across my knuckles making my pussy wet.

"My name is Nikki. would you like to dance?" I ask flirtatiously.

"I refuse the night to pass without you being in my arms," he answers leading me to the dance floor.

"He smiles, kisses my ear lobes and swings me around until the song stops."

He walks back to the bar and I ask for his cell phone.

"Why?"

"To let your wife know she is replaced."

"Go ahead. The only person answering is my housekeeper."

"Housekeeper huh? What do you do for a living Mr. Corbin?"

"I am a district attorney."

"Mr. Corbin, how about we exchange numbers."

He hands me the phone and I store my name as Future Wife. He sees the title and a big grin comes across his face.

I walk back to my seat and finish the evening.

I look at the phone and see I have a missed call from an unknown number.

"Necole you could have answered the phone."

"Nikki I didn't hear it. You probably left it on silent again."

"Someone called me from this number."

"Yes this is Benito. I apologize for leaving the restaurant earlier but I had an issue to handle. I would like to see you if possible."

"Sure, I will text you the address and meet us around 11:30 pm."

"Ok I'll see you then."

"And I'll see you eating me."

Chapter 9

Asperilla

Ladies, thank you for arriving on time. It stops me from dragging you bitches by your hair. Let's discuss the party.

"Asperilla I was hoping a little bit of your old ways were tucked away in a new personality," Cherry says.

"Fuck it, I'm still ruthless! They should have casted me as the first female gangsta of *N.W.A*. Stop interrupting me before I have you tricking with the new pastor of the church."

"Asperilla that shit ain't funny. You know I went through a lot."

I chuckle knowing she had a rough time but I enjoy getting under her skin.

"Okay Cherry I'm done."

"Ladies, the Captain wants to spend his settlement on this party. We are giving the best gift known to man. Pussy!"

The ladies shout, "Wet Pussy!"

"Ya'll need to milk them dry and ride their dicks until it breaks."

"Jaz you are the main focus for the Captain. You will be handcuffed with a hidden key in your clothes."

"Be prepared for enormous drinking and twisted minds throughout the night. Remember to stay level headed and don't sip or smoke anything from them. This party will be packed but twenty-five men have paid for the outer world experience."

"The first experience is a shower room equipped with tables." I wink at the eight Korean ladies.

"They will tranquilize them with a shower and dick massage. These muthafuckas will be drained and fresh. Any questions before I continue?"

The ladies didn't say a word.

"Okay good!"

"The second experience is a strip tease performance. Hard dicks, dripping pussy, bouncy titties and half of them won't survive the erotic gauntlet; then the nudist gallery.

"All aboard, next stop is the edible buffet. Grapes, strawberries, pineapples and scrumptious ladies. Please do not be alarmed if they pour champagne on your body and suck it."

"Damn Asperilla! This is out of control. I might need an oxygen tank," Kandi says.

"I told ya'll to expect a wild night but the money is worth it. Where the hell was I?"

"Last phase is the Chamber of Wetness. The chosen ones will fuck the sight out of their eyes and one more thing."

"Tadow!" pulls out the naughty cop uniform including buttoned front dress, hat, fingerless gloves, tie, belt, netted thigh high stocking, heels and walkie talkie."

"Hell, that uniform is sexy as fuck," Jaz says.

I glance at my watch. Where the hell is Malakai?"

I am ready to dismiss the meeting when he strolls in.

"Good evening ladies, how is everyone doing?" He asks.

He kisses me. Damn that's odd. First time he's affectionate around the ladies. This is a greeting I will reverence.

Malakai

"Asperilla gave you the blueprint. It will be held at the *Tampa Palms Golf and Country Club* and cameras will be in every room for your protection. One last pleasure ride to never work hard again. I can't make you leave the game but you have been taught to survive on the streets, go to school or get a legal job."

"Ladies take the night off, rest and tomorrow is back to business."

I escort the ladies to their cars and watch them leave.

"Malakai," she moans.

"Yes Asperilla, how can I serve you?" I say and kiss her soft lips.

She breaks my kiss and replies, "Time to prepare for the wedding after the retirement party."

"Baby please forgive me. I lost track of time."

"Malakai I have another request."

"Asperilla, I am listening."

"There is a young woman on the streets. She has a man pimping her for pennies."

"What do you want to do?"

"Save her."

"Why have you taken an interest in her?"

"She reminds me of a younger version of myself."

"I'm not going to ask how the hell you know about this situation and why are you on that side of town?"

"You know I get bored and ride through the hood sometimes."

"Her man won't let her go without a fight. That's his bread and butter."

"We have to buy her freedom."

"Wow I am impressed Asperilla."

Caressing her face, "You are right and I am willing to help you."

"Thank you baby! You are amazing. I could do it but I would shoot first and ask questions later."

"I know; we don't need another murder. Let's go upstairs and have a calm evening."

She points to her pussy and blurts, "Only thing I need calm is your tongue. You can sleep in my pussy. Fuck a dog house."

I fireman carry her to the bedroom and ease her to the ground.

She looks at me and asks, "Jacuzzi or shower?"

"Sucking clit under a perfect moon? Jacuzzi." I respond.

"Strip and meet me outside. Time for cum and rum."

Ending the evening with my face buried between the perfect place on Earth.

Chapter 10

Nikki

"Necole! Benito texted saying he will be here any minute."

"Do you want to fuck him first or shall I let you enjoy my leftovers."

"Bitch you always go first, old selfish ass. I don't know why you are teasing me by asking that bullshit."

"I know right; I was fucking with you. You should have known after two years of being dickless that I was going to jump on it. There is no need to worry. after I nut down his throat and let him fuck me in a couple of holes; you are free to do whatever you want."

There's a knock at the door, "Hurry up and change clothes Necole."

I look through the peep hole to ensure it is Benito, open the door and greet him with a kiss.

He declares, "Damn I can get use to this type of greeting."

I want to tell him that he's only a nut and will be forgotten tomorrow.

"I ain't got shit else to say to you. I want to fuck."

He smiles and asks, "Will the other woman be joining us?"

"No, she will come in later. You are all mine. Follow me to the bedroom and let's celebrate a wonderful evening."

I get him to shut up and listen. Damn some men talk too much.

"Get undress and make yourself comfortable," I say.

I reach under the bed and pull out my restraints. After I grab everything, I take off my yoga pants, boy shorts and tank top.

"Nikki you are a delicious specimen."

"Thank you Benito. you are about to be tied and fucked."

I am expecting him to have a comeback but he didn't say a word. I see his dick is ready and has the sexiest vein on the left side. I wasn't going to suck his dick but let Necole do the head doctoring. I might have to prepare my throat for surgery.

I end my fascination and crawl on the bed; making my way to his wrists. I strap him nice and tight. The icing on the cake, I pull out the blindfold, tell him to play nice and be rewarded double for his pleasure. Benito obeys my command and I rejoice when a man submits.

"Benito open your mouth and make your tongue wave for me. Good boy. Don't say shit during this session but you can moan all you want. Another thing, don't cum unless I ask you too."

"Yes Ma'am."

"Bitch what I say," slapping the shit out of his face. "Listen Benito, don't say anything."

He nods his head and I am ready to proceed with a long overdue nut.

I position my pussy over his mouth and chew on his balls. Damn I am getting stimulation after being neglected for two years.

Benito works his tongue slowly across my lips and once the tip ease over my clit, I bit his dick from the orgasmic shock. I keep my composure, rub the tip of his head and open my throat.

He has a fetish for pinching. Every time I suck him down; his nails dig in my cheeks like ant bites. My ass will be red in the morning but I'm not telling him to stop. I pounce on his face while swallowing his dick deeper and deeper. This shit feels good and I'm going to flush his face.

"Benito! Don't stop tongue fucking me."

"Eat all of this pussy!"

"Dig all the juices out!"

I plow my head down and suck his dick as fast as I could while stroking it up and down. I am determined to have a geyser explode in my mouth but he will drown in this waterfall.

His face is taking a beating since he can't use his hands to throw me off. I'm going to break his nose. I stop sucking his dick and lick the tip while stroking the shaft.

Benito tongue stroke is identical to a miner digging and clawing through a cave searching for air. This man is a wilder beast with oral skills.

He moans louder. He bet not fuck up the ambience. His sounds provoke me to stroke harder as I lick. Craving to taste his cum; flickering my tongue in a rattlesnake motion across his mushroom tip until the first one spurts out.

Even though he is cumming, I deep throat it all. He slaps my ass multiple times as a signal for me to stop.

I spin around, grab the head post and sit on his face. I am going to suffocate his ass until I get my nut. Where is this muthafucka; it has been two years?

"Oh shit. I can feel it now."

The bed rocks and I lock my thighs against his head preventing his squirm. I ride harder and harder until I feel a tingle in my clit.

"Benito, hold still baby."

It didn't take long between riding and his sucking until I squirt over the blindfold and his face.

"Aww Yes. Aww Yes."

I release the bedpost, slide down and commence to riding. Place my hand on his chest, squeeze his nipples and rotate my hips.

He has never been fucked this way and I had to scream for him to thrust back.

He caught on as he hits the right spots with force unspeakable. I am going to cum faster than I did when he was eating.

I slap his face a few times and scream, "Fuck me Benito."

Every slap makes him angry and I am delighted because I need him to fuck the shit out of me. I pounce up and down repeatedly until my juices run all over him. I collapse to my knees and lay on his chest for a second.

I whisper, "Please give me a second. Whew! It's hotter than hell in here."

I catch my second wind, tell him to relax and I'll get my sister for the second round. He smiles and I know he is eager to see what she has in store for him.

I announce, "I'll change your blindfold. Damn this is soaked with juices."

I search the dresser and pull out a red laced one. I place it around his eyes, kiss his lips and tell him that she will be in shortly.

"Benito I want you to know that she has her own set of rules and you need to do everything she asks. He nods his head in obedience like a trained house dog."

My pussy throbs from riding since I haven't been fucked in a long time. I need an ice pack on my shit but I feel wonderful.

I leave the room to get Necole. I know she is wondering what is taking me so long to tag her in but it's not my fault; the first nut took forever.

"Necole where are you?"

She is not in the backroom. I peep in the bathroom and she is in the shower.

"What the hell are you doing?"

"I heard all the noise you were making so I decided to play in my pussy until we switch."

"Well you don't need to play anymore. There's dick in the room and get out the way so I can wash his scent off me."

"Was he worth it?"

"He will do for now. Now stop worrying and let Benito suck your pussy out."

Necole

I haven't seen a dick since my husband was killed and I vowed that I wouldn't fuck another man unless it was Malakai but I am horny. Nikki probably had him eating her ass; I might need to wash him. I enter the room and smell the sex musk from the first episode.

"How are you doing Benito?"

I can tell Nikki told him not to speak but I want to hear his voice. I need to know who the hell I am with before I fuck him.

"Benito you can speak; I am not my sister."

"Thank God. I wanted to ask for a drink of water ten minutes ago."

"Yes, Nikki can be dominant. Relax, I'll take care of you."

On my way to the bathroom I thought about all the guys Nikki and I shared. We have done some wild and crazy shit and they always come back begging for more.

I grab a soapy washcloth to clean my sister juices off. There hasn't been a man in our presence in a long time so he will have to accept smelling feminine tonight.

I turn the faucet off, return to bed and wipe his dick. He lets out a small moan that is delightful and sexy.

"Are you okay?"

"Yes. You caught me at a brief sensitive moment."

Wow! He has a nice dick with beautiful balls and shaven. I wash while rotating them in my hands.

After the last wipe, I lick the side of his dick, roll my tongue on the tip of his head and take a deep slurp.

He releases a sexual gasp during my oral performance and I know he is ready to fuck. I pull his dick out my mouth and kiss his face. He opens and tickles my tongue.

His kisses make me wetter and hornier so I break away and asks, "Are you ready to eat my pussy? I will only untie you to eat and finger me until I cream down your fingers. Can you handle that?"

He replies, "That's not a problem and would enjoy every minute."

I roll off the bed and unloosen the restraints. He grabs me immediately and throws me on the bed.

"So you want me to finger fuck and suck you out?"

"Yes muthafucka! Do it and keep the blindfold on."

He couldn't have eaten tonight because he was gnawing on my clit equivalent to a tiger with fresh meat. I grab his head, spread my legs wider and thrust my pelvic into his face.

"Benito eat all of this juicy pussy. Slurp on my clit. Finger my asshole."

I am throwing the right commands. He doesn't say anything but I will bless his throat.

Gravitating his fingers inside my asshole deeper and deeper. The view of him eating my pussy blindfolded is outrageous.

"Oh fuck yeah! Eat this pussy."

Benito turns me into Spiderman; climbing walls in this muthafucka.

I'm going to shoot all types of webs in his mouth. They say with great powers come great responsibility and I'm going to cum with all of the authority invested in me.

"Dammit! Oh shit."

He has three fingers in my asshole; sucking and blowing on my clit simultaneously. This shit is beyond what my ex-husband used to do. I push my pussy towards his face to suck the wetness as his tongue vibrates on my clit.

I throw my head back and enjoy the pleasure of ass fucking by watching my legs in the buck. I'll erupt on the sheets and Nikki can wash them.

"Benito."

"Yes."

"Pull your tongue back slowly and fuck my ass with your fingers."

"Whatever you like baby."

He withdraws slowly, leaving his fingers in my ass while I squeeze my clit.

"Keep your fingers in but stand over my face so I can suck your dick."

You didn't have to tell him twice. I open my mouth to receive my gift. Precum touches down first; devouring his inches while flickering my clit back and forth.

He fucks the shit out of my throat. I want him to bust all of his juices but he better hurry before I squirt my river.

He picks up the pace of fingering my ass and pumps his dick faster.

"Aww Fuck I'm about to cum," he shouts.

I slam my hips up and down over the bed. My legs shake and a few swipes across my swollen lips, I explode. He has experienced the true meaning of Slobberknocker.

"Ohh shit! Here I cum baby. Here I cummmmmm."

After hearing those words, cum swishes through my mouth like traveling in the tunnel of love. He cums, collapses on my chest and breathing hard as hell.

"Fuck that! Benito get your ass up."

"Damn can a man rest? I have been slanging and eating all night."

"Well roll the fuck over and I'll be right back."

I knew I should have gone first. Nikki always draining muthafuckas energy but Benito will fuck me tonight. I bet Malakai wouldn't ask for rest. I know exactly what I need to do.

I run to my bedroom, grab Malakai's picture and return to the room.

"Benito," I shout.

"Yeah."

"I hope your dick is able to last about three to five minutes. I need you to rip my pussy while I am on my knees. Can you handle that?"

"Three to five, sure Necole or whatever games you all are playing. Ya'll sound the same anyway."

"You are a dumb muthafucka. We are identical twins but I bet we don't suck dicks the same. Get your ass up and fuck the dog shit out of me. If I call out the wrong name, don't stop."

"What the fuck!"

"Quit being a bitch and do it."

"Ya'll are into some crazy shit but whatever."

"Keep the blindfold on. Don't want you looking at my man because you will never be able to fuck better than him."

I climb in the bed, spring to my knees and hold the picture inside my hand.

It didn't take long for Benito to get inside of me. I hear him talking shit but I tune his ass out and focus on the picture.

"Damn Malakai, you are a sexy muthafucka. Beat this pussy! It's yours. Fuck me Poet!"

I bring the picture closer to my face; kissing and licking as I envision Malakai fucking my brains out.

"Oh Shit, I love your words. Fuck me. I'm your slutbucket. I can't believe I am getting this dick after waiting so long. Got Dammit! I want to feel it in my stomach."

I bury my face into the picture and take it. This nut will not take long since the strokes are harder and deeper with each thrust. I feel a slap on my ass.

I scream, "Slap it again Malakai."

He does it more and I am ready to cum. I clench my lips on his dick and he loves it.

"Malakai! Please bust on my ass."

His tempo gets faster and my nut is almost there.

"Ahh, Ahh, Ahhh. Malakai I'm cumming all over your dick."

I scream, "Pull out and cum on my ass cheeks."

He wets my cheeks with poetic cum. I lie there for a minute as it rolls down to the side of my rib cage.

I open my eyes from my pleasurable moment and gets pissed coming back to reality.

I toss him off, "Clean up and get the fuck out. You got your nut. Whatever issues you have, take it up with my sister. She is the one that invited you. You can play by our rules and hope to get another chance or leave and never return."

I exit the room and close the door.

Fucking Benito only made me want Malakai more. I punch a hole in the hallway and go in my room to sleep off my frustration.

Chapter 11

Necole

It takes forever to fall asleep while thinking of Malakai. I should be in his arms instead of that bitch. She thinks she is a diva or something; always flaunting and bragging about her position.

I enjoyed the vision of being fucked doggy style; my pussy and sheets were soaked with excitement.

I take my morning stretch, roll out the bed and into the bathroom. This shower will not only clean my body but my mind from the thoughts of last night. Nikki is always on another level. I'll surprise her with breakfast for last night's adventure.

The water feels great as I unhook the faucet head and plant my foot on the shower wall. It's a beautiful thing having the pleasure of bending my head and watching the water drip down my clit. This shit is arousing and I shouldn't masturbate but fuck it. Increase the water pressure, stick two fingers in and slide back and forth as the water stings my velvet tip.

"Oh Shit! This muthafucka coming early."

Pull my fingers out, place them in my mouth and suck on them for fun. Wet sweet pussy should be an ingredient for cake batter. Enjoying the essence for a few seconds before slowly sliding them back inside of my hole.

I better get this nut before my foot slips and I bust my ass. Sometimes you have to encourage yourself and all my motivations are in my fingers.

"Damn, Ugh, Ugh, Ugh, Ugh."

I came and juices run down my fingers, drops the shower head and it bounces. I pull my foot from the wall, catch my breath and slowly place it on the stand.

"Whew! I am ready to start my day. A bitch is ready for an omelet and bacon now."

I grab my *Philosophy's Falling in Love* shower gel and massage my skin from the morning dew.

I can't stay in here forever besides Nikki will wonder what is taking me so long. Rinse my body, turn off the faucet and lotion up.

Today is one of those I don't give a fuck days; jogging pants, no panties and a tank top. I doubt if we are going anywhere so I'll be fine and head into the kitchen.

Nikki sits in the chair with legs cross sipping tea resembling a high and mighty bitch from England.

"What the hell you doing up so early?"

"Someone had to make sure Benito left this morning."

"I'm sure he was safe producing sounds in your pussy before he left."

"Indeed he did. Don't turn all of this on me because he said you was acting looney by bringing out pictures and shit."

"Is it a crime to be fucked face down while staring at the man I love? Fuck Benito! He should be happy he had a chance to get a piece of this pie."

"Are you hungry Nikki?"

"Bitch I'm starving."

"Why haven't you cooked?"

"Because I was waiting on my beautiful sister to get out the shower and do it."

"You are lucky I love your ass; anyway I am thinking about an omelet and bacon. Would you like one?"

"I'm so hungry that I would eat pussy wrapped in a burrito."

"You are crazy as hell but I'll do the bacon."

I open the refrigerator and grab all of the ingredients. I turn around and Nikki looks strange. I hate it when she gets quiet.

"Nikki what's on your mind? I am tired of you looking deranged."

"I am fine just going over the plans in my head to get you and Malakai together."

"What about the money?"

"Yeah I am getting to that. I don't care about his money. I believe I have found something better. You remember that fine white guy Corbin."

"How could I forget the way you two were dancing?"

"Whatever, Necole. I decided to slowly focus on his money and get you with Malakai; we both can have what we want."

"How the hell you know he is going to call you?"

"Trust me. Stop staring at me and flip that omelet."

I shift my attention to the stove, finish the last touches on the food, grab some plates and serve breakfast.

"Nikki it's doesn't matter if he calls or not. I'm delighted that you are here."

"Thank you sis! This is why I love you. Who do we kill first, Charles or Joselyn?"

"Damn I give you a compliment and you smile in my face and then want to commit murder in the same breath. Eat your breakfast before it gets cold and afterwards we can discuss who dies first."

"Umm this omelet is freaking delicious. What the hell you put into it?"

"Everything except the pussy you requested."

"Oh shit! Lil sis wants to be a comedian this morning."

"Naw, I want to put plans into actions and move toward the bigger target."

"Now what did Benito say on his way out this morning. I know he is coming back because being tied is his forte."

"Girl who are you telling, he was the perfect subject. I have something for him on the next round."

"Next round! Are you forgetting about Mr. Corbin already?"

"Hell to the Naw! I don't want him to see my wild side yet. Once I get what I need from Benito, I will focus harder on him."

"Nikki, you are a dirty bitch and I love it."

"Necole, thank you for breakfast."

"After a goodnight's fuck, it's the least I can do."

She helps clean the kitchen and finish our conversation. I probably would have given it to Charles first but that orgasmic fuck from Benito and Malakai's picture sparked a flame inside of me.

"Nikki, I want that dress from Joselyn. She can continue to breathe as long as she plays nice."

"I hate to bust your perfect bubble but a thot always looking for sex, money and drama. I'll try it your way and see what happens."

"Thank you for listening. I'll demand it's in her best interest to return it."

"I'm not going to laugh at you, yes the fuck I am."

I watch Nikki laugh until tears fall from her eyes. I don't understand why she thinks I am naive or lost in my thoughts.

"For the record Nikki, I am only thinking about you and making sure you stay out of trouble."

"I'm sorry sis but you are funny as fuck at times."

"Anyway! What are we doing today?"

"I'm down for whatever you decide."

"We should have popcorn and watch a movie in bed."

"Which one?"

"It's a toss-up between *Chocolate City* and *Magic Mike XXL*."

"Necole you truly know how to rattle a girl's cage. I guess we can go with *Magic Mike*."

"I preferred to watch it anyway because *Channing Tatum* is a beast. The way the trailer went with the welding helmet and he was popping dick all over the place."

"Nikki! Hurry up and get the popcorn."

She takes too long so I grab the bag and throw it in the microwave. I tap four minutes and realize Nikki shaking her head at me.

"What!"

"Necole you are on another level. That's all."

"I can't help it, I am excited. You can act nonchalant but it's written all over your face."

I hum the beat to *Pony* by *Ginuwine*, place my hand on my chest to make it pop and rise. I bring a smile to Nikki's face but the microwave went off.

"Necole get the damn popcorn so we can enjoy this damn movie."

"I'm getting it. Hold your mule!" As I pour the fresh scented popcorn into a bowl.

"Ok Nikki, everything is ready."

She turns around and walks to the bedroom. I follow behind her still humming with our movie snack.

Chapter 12

Malakai

We play undercover vigilantes on *Nebraska Avenue* in the middle of the night. I haven't been on this side of town in years. I don't know how the hell I let Asperilla talk me into this crazy shit. I hope this dude takes the money and give us the girl.

I didn't want anyone to notice my car so I bought a 1996 Honda Accord.

Asperilla grins from ear to ear since her pussy drips from being in a dangerous neighborhood.

"Do you see her?"

"No Malakai. I know she is out here somewhere."

"You said the same shit last week."

"Malakai don't make me cuss your ass out."

"Listen, let's drive down the road to that hotel. I got a strange feeling she might be there or someone will know where she is."

"What make you so sure, Mr. *Poetic Whore*?"

"It's not about being sure; it's about positions in the game. He is a penny-pinching ass pimp or boyfriend and every man need a base station.

"Asperilla, I'm saying we should drive to the *Oaks Motel* because if she is good as you say I guarantee he is trying to exhaust all the money from her. What's her name again?"

"I'm not sure about the real name but she answers to Juicy Fruit."

"What the fuck! Damn that's an original name for a hoe. She must have a gushy mouth."

"Malakai your ass is silly. Let's do this shit and return home alive."

We arrive to the hotel and all types of creepy crawlers are out. I'm talking about junkies, old strippers from the 80's and low budget dope dealers. This is worse than being in a lion's den, buck naked with meat tied around your ass. I shake my head, grab my *Glock* with the silencer and tell Asperilla this shit won't be easy. Strap up and be prepared to shoot if this muthafucka talks out the side of his neck.

"Malakai I stay ready and you know I was born for this shit."

I search *Backpage Tampa* on my cell and continue my search until I find her name.

Damn lil ma ain't half bad. She must be a little slow or maybe in love because there is no way I would have her listed with $40 sloppy top specials.

Dial the number and she picks up on the second ring. "Hello."

"Yes. I am calling to see how much are donations?"

"Are you affiliated with law enforcement?"

"No I'm not."

"Are you looking for a quick stay, half or hour."

"All I need is a nut so a quick stay will work."

"My quick stays are $40 and mouth massages only."

"Your ad says you are near Nebraska. I'm about ten minutes out."

"Ok, I'm at the *Oaks Motel*, call before you arrive," and she ends the call.

Asperilla looks at me with disgust and says, "For a man that only fucks with high class bitches; you are still a whore."

I smile and responds, "Pay attention and watch the operation. Check your phone, I'm calling you now. Keep it on speakerphone.

I can get into Juicy's head but the longer it takes, the more nervous she will become. She will signal her pimp and please beat him to the door."

"I'm ready baby."

I plant her lips with a kiss and she exits the car.

I call Juicy and she asks, "What type of car are you driving."

"I am driving a Honda Accord and be there in a minute."

I pull in the parking lot, she verifies I am in the car and tells the room number.

She hangs up and I glance at a dude on the side of the building. He smokes a blunt and plays with his cell. I knock on the door and hear a soft voice telling me to come in.

"Leave the donation on the table."

"Forty right."

"Yes."

I pull out one hundred dollars and speak, "Juicy I don't have all night, let's cut to the chase. What if I told you that I can take you away from this life of roach motels and dirty dick men?"

"You have a lot of nerves. Do you know how many men have said that shit?"

I pull and throw out nine one hundred dollar bills on the bed.

"My money talks green not shit. Now are you ready to listen."

I know she is afraid and probably didn't notice I saw her send a text to her pimp.

She laughs, rolls her tongue out and responds, "How about you get some of this Juicy Fruit."

I know she is trying to distract me by give her man enough time to knock on the door. She continues to tempt me until she hears it opens.

She jumps and yells, "Shit we talking too long."

Her theatrical emotions change when she looks up and sees Asperilla with a gun to her man's head.

"Welcome to the party."

"Who the fuck is you?"

"Keep your voice down before I cut your damn tongue out. I'm here to offer you the deal of the century. I should kill both of you for trying to rob me. I want to buy Juicy out, let's talk."

"I'll switch Juicy out for your bitch," he jokes.

Before he finishes his last chuckle, Asperilla pistol slaps his ass.

"You are not equipped to handle the pussy I fuck. Final offer, $10,000; take it or leave it. Juicy, you are leaving with us."

"What are we going to do with him?" Juicy asks.

"Let his ass go."

I pat him down, pull out his *.22 caliber* and hand it to Asperilla.

"Asperilla, take Juicy to the car."

"Have a seat man. What's your name? Oh, you are going to be hard to the very end."

"I bet you ain't shit without that gun."

I really want tonight to end well but this dude is whacking my nerves.

"Look I don't have any beef with you but you are a dumbass to turn down money. You have a lovely woman tricking in nasty ass hotels with grimy ass niggas. I know you haven't made close to $10,000 off her in months. I suggest you take what's left and never look for her again."

"You better kill me before my boys haunt you down, take my woman back and trick out your bitch."

"Do I look worried?"

He looks at my face and says, "You are that damn poet. Fuck you!"

"Yes I am and you are another dead man."

I pull the trigger. First bullet sinks in his chest and the other one to the dome. Step over his body, collect everything and meet Asperilla outside.

Asperilla has the car running when I jump in the driver seat.

"You know he will come looking for me," Juicy states.

I look in my rearview mirror and replies, "Unless he is coming back like Jesus I doubt it."

She places her hand over her mouth and sits back in the seat.

Asperilla looks over and whispers, "My pussy is leaking from the thrill of the kill. You better be ready to fuck tonight."

Chapter 13

Nikki

People should be careful about posting on *Facebook*. I befriended Joselyn two weeks ago and she checks in with her location app constantly. Today I followed her home from the store and didn't have to hire a detective or lose sleep.

I park next to her driveway, turn the radio down, look over at Necole and tell her that we are here.

"Necole, what makes you think this woman is going to give up the dress. I am sure the cum stains have turned into dried fossil shit.

"Nikki I told you before I want to inhale the semen he planted. If I could break in his house and sniff Asperilla panties, I would."

"Let's see if you can politely ask and she hand it over to you."

She smiles and says, "I will be back with the dress."

She hops out the car and struts like she's *America Next Top Model*. I shake my head, turn up the radio and lean back in my seat. Necole always thinks the world is nice but today she will find out the ugly truth.

I feel my phone buzzing in my console and it is from an unknown number. It's probably Charles punk ass. I'll give him a good blessing for fucking with me this morning. Necole and I need to eliminate this muthafucka and quick.

"Hello!"

"Wow, is this how you answer when a man waits a week to give you a call?"

"Corbin is this you?"

"Yes and I apologize for not calling sooner but my schedule is hectic at the beginning of the month."

"Corbin, please forgive me. I thought you were someone else."

"Nikki no need. I am the present and the past is behind you."

"You are as cocky as you look."

He laughs and says, "I have some free time, do you want to go out?"

I won't let him know I'm feeling him so I will play hard to get a little while longer.

"Corbin you aren't ready for a woman of my virtue so you better be ready for what I am offering."

"I was ready after you typed wife as your contact name in my phone."

I love his demeanor. I can talk to him forever but not today.

"Corbin, I accept your date. I want to go somewhere romantic and adventurous."

"Done. I will call you back within 24 hours."

"Corbin you have my attention. I'm not the type to sit around and wait on a man; don't take forever."

We share life stories for a minute and losing track of time because I forgot about Necole.

"Corbin we have to finish this call later."

"Indeed we will. Stay beautiful my future wife."

"Corbin I am the present, you better look for my ring."

"Thanks for calling me."

I hang up the phone, roll down my window and no sign of Necole. After stepping outside the car, I see her walking from the house without a dress.

She gets into the car and says, "I am ready to go home."

"Necole, you are crazy if you think that I'm going to leave without a dress especially since you had me stalking her for two weeks."

"She had some of her friends over. as soon as I mentioned the dress belonged to me; she slammed the door in my face and told me to get the fuck away from her house."

"I told you that thot wasn't going to hand it over. Sit your ass down and wait on me to come back with the dress. Matter of fact, we need to switch sides. keep the car running because it's about to get turnt up in *Carrrollwood*."

"Nikki please be careful; they told me if I come back they will beat me to sleep."

"Necole you have gotten soft since you were married to Johnathan. You need to put your big girl panties on or find some balls. Fuck them bitches. I'll get it so we can get the hell out of here."

I retrieve my bat out the trunk and knock on the door. I swing as soon as it opens. I connect it to her head on the first blow. I didn't wait to see her fall when I attack her two friends. I know I broke a rib or two and damn it feels good to beat some ass.

"You talking shit to my sister. Talk to me. I can't stand ya'll Barbie looking bitches. They are watching *Raven Symone* on *The View*. I swing across the flat screen because that hoe gets on my nerves too. I admire my work for a second, crack a smile and step to Joselyn.

"Bitch, where is the dress?"

I dig the butt of the bat in her abdomen. "Now don't make me ask again."

She points toward the bedroom but I don't trust them. Looking through her kitchen drawers and lucky for me, I find duct tape. I secure their legs, arms and a special piece for their mouth.

I rummage through her bedroom and Joselyn had the dress hanging next to the closet. She should have sold it and I would've fucked up someone else. I look at the dress and notice dried cum stains; Necole is as retarded as these hoes. Malakai's dick can't be worth all of this drama.

I grab the dress, walk out the room and pull the duct tape from Joselyn's mouth.

"Listen, it's in your best interest not to tell a soul about what happened. If you hadn't been mean to my sister, you wouldn't have gotten your ass kicked."

I put the duct tape back and kiss it to leave the lipstick as a reminder. I have pumped enough fear into their hearts until calling the police is a death sentence.

I bounce out the door with my bat, look back and say, "Stop watching *The View*. You all need to watch the *History Channel* or something."

I skip down the driveway and sling it in the back seat.

"Please be careful Nikki."

I ignore her ass, put my shades on and tell her to drive. After going through that drama to get it, she should be grateful.

"How did you get the dress?"

"Not your damn way and what difference does it make? You got it."

Chapter 14

Asperilla

"Isabella, get up and pack so we can make it to the airport on time. You have overstayed your welcome. I am tired of feeding and clothing you. You are lucky I have changed because your sweet mouth would be used at the retirement party."

"Damn Asperilla, is this how you treat la familia?"

"This is how I treat la familia who runs away and uses her mouth as a shelter for homeless dicks. You are only 19, what the fuck were you thinking? "I send money to Aunt Sofia every two weeks for your college tuition but you work at a fucking roach motel. Are you on drugs or something? How the hell you get here? I lied to my fiancé because I was embarrassed to admit you are my cousin, first cousin at that. Now I'm going to ask you again, how the hell did you get here?"

"Asperilla it's a long story, I hate when you are upset. Please calm down and I'll tell you. I didn't run away. I went to Spring Break in *Miami* with some friends. I met a sexy, thuggish and charming man. One thing led to another, we smoked, fucked then I was kidnapped and brought to *Tampa*. He told me if I called anyone or spoke to the police, he would kill me. I'm sorry Asperilla. I didn't mean to disappoint you."

"I'm not disappointed Isabella. I was hurt seeing you on *Backpage*. Malakai tells me the business will bring revelation to your front door and I'm understanding it now."

"Are you getting out the game Asperilla?"

"Not yet, I have a party to plan. You catching me in a tear jerking moment. Go shower before you work for me."

"You are joking right?"

I refuse to give an answer if I am joking or not. The truth of the matter is her cock monster could be the life of the party but my Auntie would kick my ass. I'm a bad bitch but she is the gutter cutter type.

I look in Isabella eyes knowing she is afraid and responds, "I would never do such a thing."

We exchange hugs and kisses. I can tell she is happy.

"Isabella, how the hell you get the name Juicy Fruit?"

"Asperilla you ain't the only one in the family with wet pussy."

I shake my head because only someone in my family would say crazy shit.

I leave the room, go downstairs to call my beautiful Aunt Sofia. I think about how she will talk my ears off; I send a text instead.

My phone buzzes back and it is Aunt Sofia replying thanks but a call would have been better. I text lol, you are right and I will later. She needs to know her daughter will call not me.

I am behind with planning this wedding; damn I'm getting married. Only Malakai proposes to a woman while eating her pussy. I'm not sure if I said yes because of his tongue or the ring. That's my future husband and he has worked his ass off to convince me every woman deserves happiness.

I turn the TV on *My Fair Wedding* and watch David *Tutera* transforms another fairytale wedding.

I should hire him and quit trying to do everything my damn self. I am wrapped into the show until I didn't hear Isabella call my name.

"Asperilla I'm ready to go home." Standing with her luggage; dressed in black shorts and a t-shirt.

"I can see you are comfortable and ready to fly; bout time!"

"Asperilla you are watching my favorite show. Are you thinking about getting?"

"Isabella I can't lie, yes we have been talking about it since last year and it's going to epic. I am sitting here thinking about what type of wedding I want. One thing is for sure, it will not be in a church. Enough talk about me, are you ready?"

"Yes I am but I am wondering if I could stay longer?"

"What the hell!"

"Yes, I can help you plan for the wedding and besides I have missed this semester anyway. I can pick up the classes this summer. What do you think?"

"Isabella you are going home and that's final."

She drops to her knees and whines like a puppy. All I can do is laugh at her looney ass.

"Isabella get off the floor and you are right. It will be nice to have family around; ones I can trust. I'll cancel your flight and tell Malakai you are my cousin. Call your Mama and tell her the news. Take your little dirty sex secrets to the grave because she will be livid if you ever tell her what happened."

"Asperilla, I want to ask you something."

I am not sure what she is about to ask but I can find a million reasons to say no.

"When you saw me on the street the first time, why didn't you save me?"

"I wanted to shoot your man and ask questions later. A year ago, I probably would have shot your ass too; maybe in the leg for not being in school."

"Oh Shit! Let me call the airline. You call your Mama."

I call *Delta* and luckily my wait time isn't long. The lady says I can use the flight as a credit for a future use. I hang up, look at Isabella and by the expression on her face, Aunt Sofia is putting in work.

She glances at me and I guess it's my turn to get the verbal abuse for not bringing her home. I put the phone to my ear and hear Spanish cuss words striking my ear drums then the nerve to say she loves me and protect her child.

She hangs up and I throw her the phone. "See the type of shit you started."

I give her a hug and say, "I love you. Take your bags upstairs and unpack."

"Do you think Malakai believed my performance in the car?"

I want to tell her yeah but his slick ass probably already knows.

I play along and blurt, "You deserve an *Oscar* or maybe a whack *BET* award."

She flips her middle finger and exits with her luggage.

It's a good thing I can rewind my show because I'm going to finish this episode before I go anywhere.

Chapter 15

Malakai

I pull in my parking space, grab my briefcase and go in the club. Monique greets me in a blue slim jacquard print business suit.

"Good Morning Malakai, how are you?"

"Wonderful." I reply pecking her cheek and sniffing her fragrance.

Her scent dances in my nose. The whore in me craves to rip her panties and feed her dick but rehab is paying off.

Pulling away I ask, "How are the numbers from last week?"

"They are superb; alcohol sales are up 15 percent and VIP rooms were maxed out. I can get the total when I go upstairs."

"No, I trust you."

"Malakai you have mail but it's different."

I close my eyes and mumble under my breath, "Which woman sent pussy photos?"

I assume it's fan mail. She points toward the duffle bag.

I look down, raise my eyebrow and imagine who possibly write letters to fill a duffle bag. Place my jacket on the chair and sort through them.

"Monique before you leave, please call and reschedule the meeting with the investors. I will be here for a while."

"Will that be all?"

"That's all. Thank you."

She stares at the letter and mentions, "Good luck," and return to her office.

I scratch my head and wonder, "Where the hell do I begin."

The first one resembles a man and woman in Crayola drawing with the words Malakai and Necole above it. The same shit after opening more letters.

I hum the twilight song, check the return address and still not making sense. I'm used to getting pussy shots, pairs of panties and videos but this is weird.

I ball the paper, shoot it in the trashcan and unhook the fastener on the bag.

Get the fuck out of here. This bitch has memorabilia from my old tour dates, CDs and pictures of other artists. A rainbow envelope stands out. I slide my hand across the flap and pull out a letter:

Dear Malakai,

There is no need for you to open any more letters because they are identical to this one. Now let's get down to business. I don't play games or waste time. I want to be your universe; you are the God I worship on bended knees. I have been chasing you too long. I'm tired of fucking all of these men and calling your name. Please don't think I'm cheating on you, call it a threesome because I hold your photo when I'm fucking them. I have swallowed cum, took it in the ass, guzzle dicks at a truck stop and all for you. I'm not turning back or departing Tampa without you. I have loved you since I heard your first CD. You can spit poetry and piss on me; I don't give a fuck. I want to be by your side forever. We have met before and I will leave more clues later.

I understand you have Asperilla right now but she will be replaced. You love teasing women with words and I'm going to be responsible for you receiving them. Every morning my prayers are God, Son, Holy Spirit, and Malakai. I'm blessing your food when I eat. We are perfect together. I am a Nubian Queen, long natural black hair, about 5'8, 160lbs. I have a bubbly ass with 34C breasts, juicy pussy, and a mouth called the Slobberknocker. Go ahead and gather your emotions, I'll wait. Ok that's long enough. I believe I have left an everlasting impression on you. I'm going to the tattoo parlor and ink my fresh shaved pussy with your face around it. Now all the men I fuck before you will know who I love.

Smooches

A huge swallow bounce in my throat, "Oh shit!"

I'm not sure how she knows Asperilla; I need to find her. Being faithful and catching drama, damn! Fucking fans goes against my beliefs.

I punch the keypad and buzz Monique.

"Yes."

"Please come here."

"Be right there."

Handing the letters through my sweaty palms, "Read this crazy shit."

She gasps after reading a few lines, "You have a modern day psycho."

"It's a requirement to find her before she disrupts my world."

She leaves the room and I dial Kryptonite.

She Knows by *Ne-Yo* blasts waiting on him to answer.

"Malakai, I haven't heard from you in a while. How's life?"

"Everything is good; being faithful except for nasty thoughts."

"What's up with the call this morning?"

"I need to tell you about a cuckoo fan and her duffle bag of letters."

"Sounds like a *Lifetime* stalker movie. I told you to get out the game and move to China."

"Kryptonite, are you with those Chinese assassins?"

"I am living the dream. You could have overseen the operation but poetry comes first but you are stressing over a woman stalking you."

"Man you are unbelievable, take you ass back to sleep; tell Meiying and Mei hello," We disconnect the call.

Every time I attempt to go legit, crazy shit happens. I'm not fond of my past but I'll be damn if I allow a woman to disrupt my future.

Chapter 16

Necole

"What the hell are you smiling about Necole?"

"I have the dress and confirmation the letter arrived to Malakai. Nikki you didn't have to write mean shit about Asperilla and me fucking men?"

"Fuck Malakai. He needs to understand we are tired of waiting."

"I hope the letter doesn't piss him off. I want him to fall in love for all the right reasons."

"You have his attention and will come looking for you."

I can't be mad at her. I changed a few words to sound pleasant, something to make him smile when he reads it.

I wave my hand at Nikki, "Bye sis, I'm going to try on the dress."

This dress is gorgeous, a purple halter with crossover bust panels extending into a non-adjustable neck strap; ruched detailing the sides, open back, cut-out midsection with crisscrossing skinny straps in front; two-piece look in the back and a high-low hem with twisted, knotted design for a sarong-like skirt. The best feature is Malakai's dried cum stains. I sniff them and wish to be closer to him. I can't wait to drink vodka cum shots. It's a shame to be obsessed however his words do it.

Snatch off my clothes, slip on the dress and admire myself in the mirror.

Oh Shit! Perfect.

I press the button on the remote to my favorite song and dance:

Don't stop, pop that, don't stop
Pop that pop that pop that (What ya twerkin' wit'?)
Don't stop, pop that, don't stop

Dropping, hands on my thighs, shaking and bouncing. I'm in the zone as I get in a hand stand. Twirl my hips, jump in the air and land on the floor to pop my ass harder. Left cheek, right and down into a split. Lean toward my ankles, throw my head back and sing:

Bitch! Stop talkin' that shit
And suck a nigga dick for some Trukfit

I love this fucking song and it makes me horny. I take the dress off before I rip a hole in it besides Nikki would be pissed.

"Damn right I will be pissed!"

"How long have you been standing there?"

"Long enough to see you twerking around the room."

"Don't stand there, help a bitch up."

After she pulls me up, I walk to the mirror to make sure I haven't torn anything.

It looks great. I slip it off and see Nikki spinning her index fingers around her head. This hoe makes the cuckoo sign like I was the one locked up.

"Nikki what's on your mind," I ask getting dressed.

She curls her lips and announces, "We need to take care of Charles."

"I'm ready but it will be done my way."

She shrugs her shoulders and answers, "Ok."

I expected a long speech about being chicken shit. I am pissed she got the dress from Joselyn. She won't always be around to protect me. I need to handle my own business.

"Nikki I will make plans next week and guarantee you will love the outcome."

I look at my watch, "Nikki, *Criminal Minds* is on."

"Hurry up," she shouts running.

I take a last peek at the dress and shout, "I'll be right there."

Maybe they will show an episode on how to kill Charles.

Chapter 17

Malakai

"Good afternoon Malakai, it's a pleasure to sit and discuss business. We are interested in your club especially knowing it was voted the best nightlife spot in *Tampa*."

"Honestly, after whipping my dick on stage I expected you to go elsewhere. Thank you for meeting with me and yes my club is home to A-lister in the city. It is our passion to produce the best to whomever step through the door."

He pulls his neck tie and announces, "$300,000 is the bidding offer."

Clearing my throat not once but twice because his offer is bullshit. I can make that amount in three months with my regular crowd.

He glances at his team, scratches his head and asks, "Was it not enough? This is why we are here to negotiate. Let's try a different amount. A quarter of a mill, rights to your clients list and an extra buy out bonus of $200,000 paid in monthly installments."

"Now you have my attention but I have a few requests if I consider. You can't change the name or allow it to foreclose."

"The main person grabs his *iPad* and asks, "Can we have a moment for discussion?"

I slip my hand in my pocket, "Take all the time you need fellas; I'll be down the hall. Call my cell."

"Monique!"

"Damn Malakai, you could knock. You startled me. How's the meeting?"

"Same old shit, rich people trying to manipulate. Hustling is my business and nothing but loyalty and respect for it. *John Cena* on their ass!"

"You are a fool."

"Indeed, I have a proposition for you."

"I'm listening."

If I leave *Tampa*, would you be interested in taking over the place. You can't have my office since I masturbate in there from time to time."

"Ewwww. You are nasty."

"Well it's my office. I am willing to give you 75% and I'll take 25%."

"Malakai are you serious?"

"Yes! Your work habits are flawless. You show up on time, stay late and the customers love you."

"How much they offering?"

"A quarter of a mill."

"That's a lot of money Malakai."

"I thought about taking it but the people make this place special. You can't put a price tag on happiness. Remember if I leave, you are first in line to take over."

"Your phone is going off."

I glance down and guess they are ready to present a new deal.

"Fellas let's drink to our success," I express entering the room. Grab the champagne glasses, and pour everyone a drink.

"Malakai, please hear our demands. The name Love Divine it's a silly name for a club. We want something sexy like Herotica."

The glass slips from my hand and shatters, "You calling my club silly; that name is sacred. Gentlemen, you have overstayed your visit. Please leave, better yet, get the fuck out!"

"Screw this! I'm delighted to get out of this dump. You have wasted our time. We could have chosen any club and you are upset over a damn name."

No one disrespects Love Divine. I retrieve a broom in the closet instead of sweeping the glass, I jab the head in his throat.

"Bitch now who's silly?"

The rest of the team shuffle their feet toward the door.

"Take this piece of shit with you before his ass goes in the trash."

They gather their paperwork, shove them in the briefcase and run out the club.

Monique runs in, "Is everything ok?"

"We had a disagreement, club is not for sale."

"I need to think about your offer?"

"I believe so."

"See you tomorrow Monique. I need a drink or a mic to calm down. Today has been horrible. Watch your step, there's glass."

"The broom is over there Malakai. Stop destroying it before I have a chance to own it."

She embraces me with a hug and hands me the broom, "Here you go Boss."

I sweep the glass and notice my phone lighting up. Damn it's Asperilla. What the hell does she wants. It better not be another save a woman from her pimp scam.

I ran the report on Juicy and found out they're cousins. I'll let her slide for now; my hands are full with a groupie.

"Hello."

"Hey love. You want to go dancing tonight?"

"Sure, you haven't been in a long time and a different atmosphere would be lovely."

"It will help clear my thoughts," I mumble under my breath.

"Wonderful. I also have a surprise when you get home."

"As long as I am not scaling walls again."

"Malakai you are too funny; you deserved everything," She giggles.

"Aight, I'll be home shortly. I love you."

"Love you too."

Chapter 18

Malakai

"Asperilla, you have applied three colors of lipsticks over 15 minutes. Who the hell are you trying to impress? I'm not sure why I agreed to this; I should be home resting after a hectic day with the investors."

She blows a kiss after the last color and utters, "Invest in this pussy. Fuck me until my orgasms crash on Wall Street."

"I'll fuck you up if you don't get out this car. Let's Go! What are we waiting on anyway?"

"If you must know Malakaiiiiiiiiii, I don't want to be the first one in class."

"Get the fuck out of here. Are you serious?" I flip the ignition, run to her side and yank the car door.

I whisper in her ear, "Let's go now before you piss me off." I echo the words slowly for 10 seconds until she understands I am not playing.

"Damn I'm ready. You play too much, get the fuck out my ear."

She gets out and speed walks ahead of me; throwing her voluptuous ass in those jeans.

"Wait up, I have one more thing to say."

"What the hell you want?"

"Be prepared to have your accent fucked from your vocals."

"Papi I love when you talk nasty," she hints squeezing my hand.

Asperilla haven't danced in a long time and everyone's happy to see her. I scan the room making sure the instructor I fucked wasn't teaching. She used to bend every way possible for me. I remember when -

"Malakai!"

"Yes!"

"Allow me to introduce Terrell; he is the new dance instructor tonight."

I shake his hands and relieved to have a male teacher. If I wasn't a poet.32 I would have been a dancer; they get pussy too.

Terrell ends the conversation and instructs everyone to grab their partners and prepare to dance. He demonstrates a few steps before turning on the music.

Asperilla starts and throws me off step. She arches her eyebrow and says, "Keep up."

Fuck that! She's not about to outdo me.

I stop her to regain my posture and status as the leader. Our fingers intertwine, placing my arms around her lower back and she throws her arm over my shoulder. We move to the music, she rolls her hips and sidesteps. Spinning her around, slide my left leg back, shake my hips and bring her closer. She gives a head nod as approval.

My knees grind on the outside of hers. I am delighted to see her blush.

She pauses and does a forward lean like *Michael Jackson*. By now the class stops and watches us.

I spin her in a circle and she twirls back into my arms. I look in her eyes and kiss.

The class shows their appreciation by clapping and whistling.

You never know the beauty of a woman until you glaze into her eyes and her energy becomes yours.

"Malakai what are you looking at?"

"Completeness!"

"Here you go again with this poetic stuff."

"Not this time, you truly complete me. I can't wait to marry you."

"Aww that is the most beautiful thing you have said in a long time. Are you taking the last name Valdez?"

"Hell naw. I want to shoot off this nut in the restroom."

"Malakai I am thinking the same thing. Male or female?"

"I'll take male for $200."

We push the door and look where to serve her.

"Malakai I'm not getting on the sink you can erase that idea," She implies.

I motion for her to come with two fingers. She twists towards me in a left over dance, drops down, unbuckles my pants and slide them down in slow motion.

"Go against the door," She commands.

She unfastens her button and wiggles her jeans off as I lift her in the air, "Don't drop me."

She is gorgeous, standing in a halter top and heels.

I lift her left leg on my shoulder trying not to trip since my pants are down, pick her up and position her pussy in my face. Tongue massaging her clit as she gyrates her hips.

Damn her juices are delicious.

"Slurp that clit Papi! Ahh Ahh. Puta! Pruébame."

Doing what she commands however I think she is calling me a bitch. I don't give a damn because I'm focusing on making her cum cover my neck.

"Malakai," She moans.

My tongue waves across her clit. She pulls her hair, lean back and slides forward and back.

Juices in my nose and I want to wear her pussy as a face mask.

"Malakai I'm about to squirt. Ohh Shit!"

The flush comes and I'm ready. I bite on her clit and she screams as she cums. After she finish, I lower her to the floor and place my shirt over the sink.

She spreads her legs and claps her ass to run my dick from behind.

She throws her head back and moans, "Fuck me."

I slap her cheeks, grab her hair into my fist and shouts, "This is my pussy."

"Yes Papi!"

"Who's pussy?"

"Malakai this is your pussy, own it."

"Take this dick."

She screams, "More, more."

My mission is fucking her out the heels, "Clinch this dick Bitch! Clinch it tighter!"

"Choke me Malakai. Choke me."

I squeeze her neck and feel my nut easing up my shaft. It didn't take long to shoot it like a missile.

"Asperillaaaaaaa, Oh fuck."

I release my seeds, pull out and admire the cream pie dripping. She sucks it in and out her pussy with a throbbing pulse.

"Malakai, go to the car and get my bag."

"I can't leave you in the men restroom."

She pulls a gun from her purse and assures, "I will be fine."

I hurriedly dress and say, "Be right back."

I hope she doesn't kill anyone before I return. I run back and she is washing her hands.

"Took you long enough. Are you washing your dick?"

"After running outside and getting sweaty, I'll take my stains home as souvenirs."

"You are such a dirty retard. Hand my pants."

"Here you go. Wait a minute. Who the hell buys the same pants?"

"I do. Never know when you might need a pair for killing or sexing."

She retouches her makeup and hair and whispers, "Another adventure to tell the grandkids one day."

Chapter 19

Necole

"Charles agreed to meet at *Lettuce Lake Park*. He said we better have all the money or he's talking to the police."

"Fuck Charles! He ain't getting a fucking dime," Nikki shouts flipping through the newspaper.

She never worries about anything but I'm nervous as hell. My hand trembles from the thought of killing him. I promised Nikki I can handle the situation.

"Nikki you are right, Fuck Charles! Fuck Charles!" I shout.

"Girl stop screaming in my damn ear," Nikki states shaking her ear lobe.

"My bad, I was excited for a minute."

"Nikki I'll be back. I have to double check my *How to Get Away with Murder* starter kit."

Cash, shovels, guns, knives, pepper spray, rope and gloves. I'm not sure if I need them however you never know. Oh shit! Where's the ax? It's laying on the floor next to the nightstand. I can't forget this; might need to chop this snitch bitch to pieces. Damn, it's 6:30pm already. Where did the time go? We have to get ready to set the trap for Charles.

"Nikki!"

"What the hell you want Necole?"

"Go in the room, grab the bag and load it up."

Nikki takes a long time to bring it, let me check on her ass.

She's giggling and making love faces on the phone, probably talking to Corbin.

"Nikki!"

She ignores me and I shout louder, "Bitch! Get your stank ass off the phone."

I toss the apple from the counter and lands against the wall where she sits.

She ends the call and says, "Throw something else at me Necole and watch me spank yo ass."

I grab the bag and responds, "Whatever, get dressed."

She places her hand on my shoulder and admits, "I am sorry."

I wish she would acknowledge Corbin has her nose wide open.

"All is forgiven Nikki." I honor her apology and walk to my room and put the money in the bag.

I load and take them to the car and on the way back Nikki stands in the kitchen dressed in steel toe boots and a bandana.

"I'm ready Necole."

This is the Nikki I love; ruthless, raw and uncut.

She grabs the bag with the cash, looks at me and asks, "Are you sure you ready for this?"

"Damn right I am. Let's go."

"Are you sure you told him the right location Necole?"

"He will be there. I promised him the Slobberknocker."

She balls her fist back and forward and states, "I know you are not about to spin his top Necole."

"Go to hell, I was willing to tell him anything to come. This is my murder and I'll plan it however I please. Sit back and watch."

She leans back in her seat and I hear the sigh coming from her breath, "Do you Necole."

I am not in the mood for Nikki shit tonight.

The trees are getting bright and my attention shifts to an oncoming car.

I snap my fingers and yell, "Clockwork baby. Every man looks for a beautiful woman with a golden mouthpiece. Stay in the car."

I'm hard and full of venom but inside is a cowardly lion. I walk to his car; heart beating faster with each step.

He opens his door and embraces me with a hug, "Damn Necole you are fine as shit. Where is your sister?" He asks displaying a sly grin.

"No need to worry about Nikki. Your attention should be all over here," I snap.

"I see ya'll on that bullshit again and the mental ward didn't help."

"Fuck you Charles!"

"Bitch the only thing getting fucked is your mouth. Hurry up with my shit."

"Charles you should really watch what you say."

"Why? Are you getting your sister to protect you? Remember I know ya'll crazy ass secret."

"Charles where is the gun?"

"Where's my money?"

"We can exchange at the bridge; I want to make sure you have the gun first."

"He pulls up his shirt, flashes the gun and blurts, "Get my fucking money Necole."

We arrive at the bridge and he didn't waste time unzipping his pants. I should pull out my knife and slice his nut sack but his dick captivates my emotions. I would kill him but my mouth wants to kill his future kids by flushing them down my throat.

"Before I slob on your cob Charles, give me the gun and count your money. You can make it rain while I'm sucking your dick and that will make my pussy wet."

He pulls his pants up, toss me the gun and says, "Shit is empty anyway."

There is no turning back, I have to do it.

He looks toward the bag, retrieve and asks, "Is it all here?"

I roll my tongue over my lips and answer, "Every last dime."

He reaches in the bag and like a rat.

Snap!

His fingers caught in a hidden mouse trap and I am not giving him a moment to retaliate. I pull my knife and stick him in the neck. His flesh sticks as it retracts backwards. I feel possessed ignoring his screams and begs for mercy. He puts up a small fight but the last pierce creates a geyser from his neck. He falls forward and the blood runs over the bridge. There is so much until I am nauseous. I drop the knife, clutch my stomach and throw up the nervousness plus lunch.

I sink my chin into my chest and eyes fill with tears, "What the hell have I done?"

"Necole, Necole."

The sound of a familiar voice but unable to respond.

"Necole get up!"

I turn my head slowly as I play a role in the *Exorcist* and accept my fate. I open my eyes and see Benito.

"Thank God," I utter.

"Where did you come from?"

"Your sister called and explained the whole thing. I'm here to help. We don't have much time."

He helps me to my feet and directs, "Go to the car. This is no place for a woman."

The walk back compared to *John Coffey* in the *Green Mile*. I am a nervous wreck, tripping over sticks and rocks along the journey, sweat pouring from my face and tingling in my toes.

I unlatch the door and my sister claps her hands together, "Congratulations Necole! You have graduated to murder."

"I feel like shit and you are having a praise party."

"Necole I took a human life, someone's son."

"Charles wasn't human. He was a snitch and you did what you had to do. Remember, this is for Malakai."

"I left the money on the bridge."

"Benito will handle everything. Let's go home."

"I can't drive right now. My clothes are bloody and my vision is blurry."

"Fine, I'll drive; slide to the passenger seat."

It didn't faze her that I killed Charles but my pulse is jumping out of my skin.

"Why did you call Benito?"

"I knew you weren't capable of being *Black Mamba* besides Benito has hidden talent in cleaning."

I bite my teeth on my bottom lip, close my eyes and pray Malakai takes me away from this nightmare.

Chapter 20

Asperilla

"Ladies, tonight we devitalize horny men and turn them into bitches. They have taken time and money from their girlfriends or wives to taste our orgasmic eruption. Do we give a fuck?"

Pumping their fist in the air and roaring, "Hell no! Hell no! Hell no!"

"Why ladies?"

"Because our pussy squirt pleasure and every man will taste it."

"You need to fuck like there's no tomorrow and no dick left erected. They will pay extra to make us stop. I want them to have thoughts of a heart attack when busting nuts. Gather your strap-ons, whips and vibrators. We were created to beat their asses and dominate. Our pussy has the power to take and create life. Now who's ready to fuck!"

"We are!"

"Why are you ready?"

Silence falls across the room as they begin deep meditation, eyes close and contracting pussy muscles. I flip my wrist to check the time, slither index finger across my neck to signal the release of their energy.

"Ahhs," fills the room like a mass choir on first Sunday.

"The floodgates are open. take your riches, crush their egos and send them back to their boring lives."

They bolt out wearing the sluttiest police uniforms needless to say the red *Louboutin* pumps are a woman's best friend.

Malakai claps his hands, "You could motivate the *Lakers* out of their losing season with your speech. I had tears running from laughing."

Cherry fans herself and gives Jaz hi-five.

"My pussy is activating superpowers right now. I have a confession and Malakai you need to hear me out too. I know this is supposed to be our last ride but it's something about taking money that increases my wetness. I can feel juices in my ass. Hold up that's my anal beads talking."

Malakai rolling his eyes, "Finish your story Asperilla. If you are doing poetry, then I'm going to continue selling pussy. Fuck baseball, Pussy is America's Pastime.

Cherry and Jaz twirl their hips, throw their hands up and sings, "No ass bitch, no backstage pass."

When Malakai is in business mode, he is such a party pooper. I flap his balls with my hand. It doesn't take long to participate and we sing,

> *We don't need no music,*
> *'cause all we wanna do,*
> *is sing and dance and party down*
> *and play with pussy too.*

Malakai smiles and says, "I will think about it." He spins around and check the computer screens with the technicians.

I whisper to Cherry and Jaz, "We are going to *Dubai* to slang pussy out the towers."

They laugh at my madness and it's a blessing we are able to get along.

"Cherry, thanks for staying and if you chose to marry Andre, you have our support. I know he makes you happy because he makes me praise my bank account on the 10th of each month."

"Jaz your ass ain't going nowhere but upstairs and fuck Captain Ramos. Fuck him nasty, no holds barred style."

She flips her hair, "I am thinking about shitting on his chest."

I scratch my forehead, "Malakai is right; something is wrong with your ass and I love it."

"Get the hell out so I can watch ya'll on the screen."

Shifting my attention on Malakai. I speak with my doll voice, cross my legs and bat my eyelashes, "Whatcha doing?"

He motions for me with one finger, "Asperilla you are getting dicked down after the party but please sit down and watch your videos."

"Yeah Yeah Yeah. I hope you gave me the best ones."

"I have the spa and shower rooms plus three. I can care less because my girls are not working them."

"Wait a minute. Damn, the Koreans are putting in work. Is this a car wash with hard dicks and hand massages?"

"Swish and Rinse."

"This shit is better than watching porn. There's jazz music playing while the ladies walk on their backs."

I run my fingers under my dress and pleasure myself.

"Asperilla what the hell are you doing?"

"I'm trying to get a nut if you wouldn't have interrupted me."

"Watch the damn videos."

"You mad because you can't beat your dick like you did in the club. Malakai look what I found."

Pull my rechargeable *Kandi Kisses* lipstick vibrator from my purse, slide it under my dress, over my lips and continue watching. I throw my left arm in the air and slow motion flip my middle finger and says, "This is for that *YouTube* video. Don't worry, I can multitask. Watch me whip and play in this pussy."

The third room has men tied to chairs and ladies lap dancing. Turn the volume up and they are, they are playing *Slow Motion* by *Trey Songz*.

I twirl my hips, push the lipstick deeper and sing, *"Oh darling, I just wanna get you out them clothes."*

These ladies deserve bonuses. One of them climbs, flips upside down with her legs hanging around his neck. She grips the pole for leverage, pull his face into her ass with her heels and twerks. She does it without missing a beat and the more her ass slams into his face it makes my pussy ecstatic. I pull the lipstick out and jab it in, out, in, out, faster and faster. I'm getting this nut and don't give a fuck who listens.

Moaning becomes louder and like a good bitch, I watch the videos as promised. My heart beats faster as it comes.

"Umm, Umm, Umm," I moan and hold my breath feeling my orgasm silently.

I give a sigh of relief, flopping back in the chair, slowly pulling the lipstick from my mound and toss it to Malakai. "*YouTube* that you bastard!"

He picks it up, sucks it and instructs me to get back to work.

My fourth room is the nude art gallery. A beautiful woman painted as a violin leaning into the arms of another woman as she positions the wand behind her back. I love it.

Everything is going well and the erotic gauntlet is successful with no issues.

"Malakai you sure you want to escape this life?"

He didn't respond but deep down he is having second thoughts.

In the last room, the human buffet; men slurp and lick the fruit off like they haven't eaten in years.

I am going to throw a gauntlet one day with a dick beating race. First one to cum wins.

The last few men makes it through and the ladies gather their things and prepare to leave. After three hours the party is over except for the officers that paid to drink from the lips of our proficient ladies.

I grab the walkie talkie, "Security, be ready as we advance towards the final stage."

Malakai flips a button and a big screen unroll from the ceiling.

He is full of surprises and better stay this way. It's a shame Isabella's missing out on the excitement. It was more than enough explaining to Malakai she is my cousin but he didn't question it.

"Malakai wassup with the screen?"

"I have to watch Jaz and the others in 3D."

"You can preach safety all day but you know you want to see ass and titties. You are such a *Poetic Whore*."

"Nah baby I'm a whore in rehab."

He kisses me, grips my ass and says, "Enjoy the show."

Flenardo

Chapter 21

Jaz

"You are naked, handcuffed and my prisoner."

He has no idea Asperilla gave me a key to break free at any time but I will entertain his demons.

He clutches his hand between his thighs, "My dick feels like a brick and I want it all in you."

I remain calm as he eases closer and closer. Twisting the key inside the cuffs to slide down my arms.

He comes closer," Bitch open your mouth."

I part my lips allowing his tongue to dance with mine. He rips my shirt, pinches my nipples and pulls my hair. I refuse to give him the satisfaction of knowing how much it hurts. I kiss him deeper and passionate as his squeezes intensifies.

"Tell me you love me Jaz," he commands.

I don't say a word then he slaps my face. I can feel the wind from the sting.

"Bitch say you love me!"

I endure more slaps before I slide off the cuff. He is busy trying to abuse me; he never notices I am free.

He pushes my head toward his balls. I lick his left ball, run my face up his thighs resembling a kitten across her master legs.

"Good pussy," he moans.

I glide back down and notices closed eyes. I snatch his balls with a quick grip and squeeze them like lemons.

Rising to my feet with his balls in my hand; he stands tip toed begging.

I whisper in his ear, "Did you miss me Daddy?"

He grimaces in pain, eyes wide, face red and I don't give a fuck.

I squeeze tighter and asks, "Did you miss this pussy?"

"Yes! Yes! I miss this pussy."

I release my grip, he falls to his knees and grabs between his legs. I fasten and lock the cuffs to his wrist.

"Get your ass on the bed like the pig you are?"

"Yes ma'am."

"All fours Captain."

"Yes ma'am!"

Lashing the flogger across his ass, "Pigs can't talk; you're a filthy animal. What they say?"

"Oink Oink."

"Lashing his ass again, again and again, "What they say?"

"Oink, Oink."

I slap his face and then backhand, "Little piggy ready to eat sloppy pussy."

"Oink, Oink."

I show my hood so he can flap his tongue across my clit, "Eat this wet sloppy pussy; eat it all."

"Yes! Yes! Ummmm."

"Put your nose in it. Snort nasty pig! Snort! I want my juices in your nostrils when you are finished."

I love making men submit to my commands,

I lean his head back and whine my pussy all over his face. Whining harder and humping in the air. He digs deeper in my pussy with his pointy nose and it feels incredible.

He pulls his nose out, licks my clit again and inserts two fingers. The joy of being eaten and finger fucked gets me wetter and wetter.

"You are my Captain Crunch, keep crunching on my pussy and I promise this nut is coming straight down your precinct. Captain, I'm going to read you your rights and you better continue serving me."

You have the right to eat this Pussy.
Any hole can be filled with your tongue.
Aww. Yes, Captain
You have the right to talk inside this pussy
If you can't afford to eat this pussy.
I will flog you until I'm tired.
You can put more fingers in my pussy at any time.
Do you understand the rights I have read to you?"

He nods, fucks me with his fingers and sucks on my clit.

I scream, "Oh, Oh, Oh, suck me baby. Shit!"

I close my eyes, cream his face and when I open; it resembles a warm *Krispy Kreme* glazed doughnut.

Remove my legs from his shoulder, flip over and grab my flogger; swinging it across his ass cheeks.

"Little Piggy likes to be slaughtered."

I swing harder and harder. Toss the flogger away, grab the keys and unloosen the cuffs. He's relieved but only for a second before I do it again and again.

"Beat your dick while I beat your ass cheeks! I'll stop when you come for me. Piggy better cum for me!"

He beats his dick harder than the stones in *Bedrock*. He grunts, "Oink, oink oink, oink."

"When you cum on this pussy, you better say wee wee. Cum Captain, milk that dick over your sweet pussy."

"Oink Oink, Oink."

He explodes milky, delicious creamy cum. I slide my legs between his and watch his emotions; huffing, puffing and sweating.

I rub it all over my pussy and moan, "Are you ready?"

He oinks in agreement.

Thoughts of wiping the cum on my toes and making him suck them but I need to get fucked.

He scoots down to free my legs. I spread eagle style and say, "Beat this pussy."

I'm flexible and want to feel dick in my stomach.

Pussy drips as he slides in and he wastes no time pounding.

"Now talk to me dirty cop. Fuck me!"

To my surprise, he doesn't say shit. I guess he is focusing on abusing my insides. For an older guy, he has the right tools; 8 ½ inches of raw dick, shave, neat and the way I love my meat.

He humps, breathes deeper and continues digging my back out. I hold my legs by the ankles and take my wonderful punishment.

"Unleash your load in me Captain."

He fucks faster and bounces his dick against my walls. He gets up, we switch positions and he lies on his back. I ride backwards and squat over his dick.

I give him the flogger and order, "Beat me while I ride your dick."

I clench his dick every time I slide up and down. The sting is pleasurable and my pussy squirts from the pain. Riding up and down, dancing with every bounce.

He releases the flogger and moans, "Jaz, Jaz, bounce that ass."

"Fuck me Captain! Fuck me!"

His thrusts match my rhythm. After 15 minutes Captain is the winner and his cum shoots like a cannon.

I flip back, stand over his face and flicker my clit across his face until I cum.

"Yes Captain. Experience my love in your mouth."

Chapter 22

Nikki

"Necole quit worrying about Charles. I promise Benito did an awesome job covering up the scene. You are not going to prison so get your ass out the apartment. It has been two weeks of you leaning sideways and dragging your feet like a zombie. If it makes you feel better, Benito chopped him in tiny pieces, fed the parts to the alligator and buried his head so deep it could be found in China. Now that Charles is out of the way, we need to get you and Malakai together. Send more letters with your pussy scent on the dress. Make sure he understands you will replace any bitch he loves. I promise you will get his attention and if he is good as they say then his ass will knock down doors looking for you."

"That's a good idea Nikki, by the way, why are you dressed up?"

"You are the one depressed, not me. I'm going with Corbin tonight and please don't blow up my phone."

"You have been hanging out with him for the past week. Can your sister get some love?"

I wrap my arms around myself and squeeze hard, "We are twins, did you feel that?"

"Fuck you Nikki."

"Necole everything will be fine. You will have your man soon."

"Thanks Nikki, you are the best."

She kisses my cheek and states, "Have fun."

I know I fed her lies but it makes her smile for a moment. I was the one locked up while she was out here with freedom. I'm tired of her obsession with Malakai.

I call Corbin, "I'm on my way."

He says, "I have a surprise for you."

I can't wait to see what he has up his sleeves.

The drive is about 25 minutes with traffic but *Chris Brown* CD gets me there; I dance in my seat to his destination. Stepping out of my car in a red *Thalia Sodi* faux-wrap dress and 5 ½ inch rhinestone platform dress sandals. I didn't walk far when a black guy in a suit greets me.

"Good Evening Ms. Nikki, I'll take you to Mr. Corbin."

I continue smiling on the inside since I didn't want him to see my expressions. He escorts me around the corner and Corbin stands next to a horse carriage. The carriage is a Cinderella style pumpkin top with cute heart decorations along the side. He reaches for my hand and kisses my knuckles.

He pulls his lips from my hand and says, "Tonight I want to fuck your mind to sleep and send your body home without me."

His line sounded similar to a romance novel I read in the hospital.

"Corbin you are a gentleman although you want to fuck my mind however my pussy is overdue for dick."

I have been talking to him for six weeks and he hasn't made a move. I hope he doesn't prefer men and if he does, he is still going to fuck me or watch me fuck someone else.

He lifts me in the carriage and announces to the coachman, "I am ready to depart with my Queen."

We ride down the streets and Corbin explains historical places as we pass.

"Nikki you look exquisite and I would drink the fragrance you are wearing."

"Do you always compliment your ladies like this?"

"Usually I fuck and send them home."

"Damn! Who would have thought you have a rough side?"

"Baby there are things you don't know but I am a refined man looking for love."

"Corbin, there are things I haven't told you. I have an ugly past."

"Nikki we all have something we regret. Don't let anything deter us from creating happiness."

He scoots closer, look in my eyes and massages my knuckles. He must be fascinated with them because he rubs them repeatedly."

"Corbin do you love my knuckles?"

"Nikki I love everything about you and your dress is gorgeous. You are amazing. I don't usually allow a woman to get close to me."

"Why me?"

"I believe we have a lot in common but what do you desire from me."

Damn Corbin, I rather fuck going down the road while everyone watches but I throw those thoughts from my head.

I respond, "I want to be loved and enjoy life to the fullest."

He looks in my eyes and says, "I am the man to kill your nightmares and birth your dreams."

"Coachman."

"Yes Mr. Corbin."

"Please stop at the restaurant, take a break and rest the horse."

Who would have thought I have gone from a strait jacket into the arms of a man who loves me deeply?

We enter the doors, music playing and we are the only couple.

I am in aww. I have never been on a date where a man showered me with balloons and a table filled with expensive gifts.

I race to the biggest box and it is designer shoes. He has them from *Jimmy Choo* to *Dolce & Gabbana*. I feel like Cinderella and he is the perfect Prince Charming.

"Corbin, how am I supposed to carry this home?"

"You can take whatever you like tonight and I'll pack the rest and deliver a gift every week until you move in."

Necole was right, Corbin has my mind all over the place and I refuse to turn this down. I'll help her with Malakai but I need my happiness as well.

"Thank you Corbin. I'll think about your offer."

He disappears into the kitchen and returns with butter pecan ice cream.

He dips the spoon in, "Please open your mouth, my love."

The first scoop is delicious; I wish nuts came with a sweet gesture.

"Nikki, feed yourself for a minute or two?"

My mouth falls open as he hands me the bowl and drops to his knees.

"Nikki every time you swallow your ice cream, I will see if I can suck it out your lower lips."

He parts my thighs and realizes I am not wearing any underwear.

"Corbin will you be able to match my sucks and licks from down there?"

He replies, "If you don't choke, I won't."

I feed myself in slow motion and his tongue proves me wrong. I am greedy and shoves the spoon in my mouth faster and Corbin matches my pace. His licks and slurps are exotic and I am going to cum.

"Ahh, Ahh, Ahh, Ahh, Ahh."

I push Corbin away and he asks, "Are you ok?"

"Yes I have a brain freeze before I could catch my nut."

"Place your tongue on the root of your mouth," he directs massaging my head.

"Damn I love his adeptness."

Partaking in a kiss, I taste my pussy on his tongue and I love me.

"Are you ready to glaze upon the star until the sunrise?"

"Corbin, I am yours, all yours. Do whatever your heart desire. I'm not going anywhere."

Flenardo

Chapter 23

Asperilla

Every little girl's dream is to wear an elegant dress captivating the audience as she floats across rose petals to the altar.

My fairy tale wedding won't happen if I can't find the dress to satisfy my happiness.

Throwing my hands in the air from frustration, "Isabella I give up."

"Asperilla everything will be alright, have faith. We'll find one."

"Fuck a dress, I'll catwalk in heels and a red lace lingerie."

She turns up her nose, "Eww I'm not coming to see booty cheeks with colorful anal beads drooping out."

"That shit would be unbelievable. Malakai can suck them before the minster says you may kiss the bride."

She stretches her hand across my face, "Asperilla you passed the bridal shop, turn around."

"Damn you are right."

I hit four quick right turns and arrive on *Westshore*. I park, race to the store and pray there's a dress I can fall head over heels with.

"Welcome to *CC's Bridal Boutiques*, home of the best selection of wedding gowns, bridesmaids' dresses and gowns for Mothers. Do you all have an appointment?"

Wheezing from the cardio, I lift my head and announce, "Yes, Asperilla Valdez."

"Welcome Ms. Valdez, please look around; there are a variety of dresses for your viewing. We'll select some to bring to your fitting room."

"Thank you."

"Isabella, I'm getting married. Let's go!" I pull her hand to help.

I scan the room and a lot of dresses scream take me. This is a difficult task. I should buy the ones calling my name.

"Excuse me Ms. Valdez, your room is ready. You can try on the dresses we picked based on your interest."

I swoop the first dress and rush into the fitting room. Dazzle by the image in the mirror, the organza and hand-beaded metallic embroidered Schiffli lace appliqués over satin is gorgeous. Flip off my shoes, unzip my pants and toss them to the side.

My eyes glaze upon my bodacious frame. "Shit! I think I gained a pound," Cuffing my 34D's, switch to the side and peeping my 23' waist and 39' thick hips.

I blow out a long breath tussling into the gown, "Whew. I am all in, time to show Isabella."

Parading out the dressing room with my arms swinging, "Isabella what do you think?"

"Aww, like a princess."

"Bitch I'm a Queen."

"Yea with your Queendom of escorts to rule."

"Damn right. Give me your honest opinion."

She glances at the other ladies and return to me, "Hmmm I love it but it's missing something. Try the second one."

The associate hands me another dress, I dash to the fitting room and strip for round two.

I close my eyes and pray, "God, let this be the one." My mouth drops when I see the image in the mirror, "Oh Shit! This is it."

Twirling and fanning the dress in the air with each turn. I am utterly fascinated by its beauty, a Tulle and lace wedding gown, trumpet silhouette with hand beaded lace appliqués placed throughout the bodice, trail down the skirt, one shoulder with crystal brooch and beaded lace strap asymmetrically adorns the back bodice, chapel length train with matching hem lace and corset.

Taking a deep and gratifying sigh, "Finally I have the dress to be married and fucked in. My pussy saturates thinking of the sexual positions we can create."

"Asperilla, hurry up. We are waiting." Isabella demands.

I strut out with an ice cream smile on my face, "Is this one?"

Isabella examine up and down and gives a thumb-up, "I told you it was the second one."

I press my palm over my eyes to prevent the tears from pouring.

"Asperilla its okay to cry. Happiness is a blessing. I'm savoring this moment because in a few minutes you may cuss someone out."

I rub my hand against my heart, "You are right. I will rejoice and be glad in it."

"Are you quoting biblical praises?"

"You know our mothers are Catholic. Don't tell Malakai; he'll probably drag me to church."

"Your secret is safe with me."

"I love this store. We will purchase the bridesmaid gowns later."

I blow a kiss at the staff, "Thanks for helping me."

Isabella points at her watch, "Hate to be a spoil sport; we are pushing for time."

"Damn, help me get out this dress."

We scurry in, transform and within ten minutes the pressure of finding the perfect dress had been lifted off my shoulders.

Once I step out the fitting room I overhear the clerk telling another woman how expensive the dresses are. I didn't mean to eavesdrop but her demeanor changed. I don't know the amount of money she has but I see sadness. I believe it's time to pay it forward and not making her suck for it.

"Isabella I'll be right back."

"Excuse me, my name is Asperilla and I'll be honored to purchase your dress for you."

Her eyes fill with joy and a double take, "You kidding me right?"

"No I'm dead serious. Save your money, have a ladies' night out at a strip club."

She leaks in my arms, "Wow! You have no idea of my excitement right now."

"When is your wedding?" I ask.

"Next month."

"Get outta here, mine too, it is a small world. I'm buying a dress and don't know your name."

"My name is Necole."

"Necole it's a pleasure to meet you. I have to join my cousin but best wishes on your wedding."

"Yours too. Thank you so much again."

Isabella lips poke out when I return, "You buying dresses for people you don't know."

"Girl shut your mouth. Let's toast with champagne. I wanted to do something nice plus I bought new clothes and shoes for you last week."

"Do I detect a little jealousy?"

"Not at all. Why is she staring? Who comes to try on dresses alone?"

I glance over my shoulder and she waves her hand imitating a *Toys R Us* kid.

"If someone bought me a $2,000 dress, I'll be looking crazy too."

"Maybe you're right. Are you buying one for me when I get married?"

"Suck ass hoe. I did a good deed. You ain't getting shit."

She slaps my ass, "I knew your niceness couldn't last."

I hesitate and wave to Necole, "Join us for a toast."

She sprints over, lifts her glass and enjoy the celebration.

"Today I am thankful and wishing many blessings on our wedding day."

We cling glasses and sip the taste of victory.

Chapter 24

Necole

A month ago frustration consumed daily living. My sister's relationship with Corbin is blossoming into something magical while I wait on Malakai. Jealousy plays a huge part. I am shifting my negative energy to meditation.

My thoughts are calmer after sitting for hours in the lotus position. It took time mastering my foot from slipping off my thighs as I chant Malakai's name.

Nikki said I was a fool for decorating my room with Malakai's photos as wallpaper, bedsheets stitched with his name and my favorite poem titles. My best picture is the one at the grand opening of his club. He held my waist and my head leaned on his shoulder. I love my creativity; Lord knows it wasn't easy to Photoshop my face over Asperilla.

Uggh, I cringe my face knowing that Babylon whore is always around. She doesn't deserve to lay next to you. Her existence will be a faded memory after I suck the power from your dick. Slobberknocker is the new Delilah and you will love me. The stars are lining up and our mental intercourse is intoxicating since Asperilla bought the dress for our wedding. She accepts her place as the side chick and if she leaves quietly, I will let her breathe longer.

I idolize my gown from her, the purple dress from Joselyn which I'm going to masturbate and send to you. Your bitches love giving me things.

"Necole who are you talking too?"

I shrug my shoulder, "I'm thinking out loud."

"I can hear you in the other room. Wow! This is my first time in here since you transformed it to a shrine."

She spins her finger outside her head, "Maybe you were supposed to be in the ward and not me."

I erect my middle finger, demonstrate the international fuck you symbol and ignore her comment.

"Necole I know you hear me. Come and talk to me when you are done with your imaginary friends."

I squeeze my fist and push out a scream, "No more negative energy in my room."

Regardless of my meditation; she always pisses me off.

I storm through the room, stomping my foot and slapping the wall. "What do you want?"

She places the teacup down and asks, "Why is there a wedding gown in your closet?"

I cross my arms, tilt my head, "Like you care what's going on in my world."

"Your mouth is good for giving brain not being smart. Necole what gives?"

"You really want to know?"

"Yea Bitch, cough it up."

"Asperilla paid for it."

She spits out her drink, "What the hell did you say."

I blow air on my knuckles and wipe my thighs, "Relax, I have everything under control. Let me explain, after Charles' death I contemplated giving up my obsession for Malakai. No man wants a scary bitch always crying, dripping snot and depending on her sister to save her. Anyway, I took a page from your book and followed Asperilla a few times last week. Two days ago I trailed her downtown as she searched for the perfect wedding dress."

"She found one at *CC's Bridal Boutiques.* She was anxious and never noticed my presence. I paid the sales associate to book an appointment at the same time. Every dress she modeled turned my stomach upside down. I walked away twice to regain my composure. Bitch had me ready to fight however I used my head and played on her emotions. I pretended the price was too expensive, flashed my sad puppy eyes and sealed the deal. She could have bought a dress from Satan and wouldn't notice. Now I have my own wedding gown to become Mrs. Malakai. What do you think about me now?"

"Sis, I'm speechless. You walked in the lion's den and possessed the key. I'm proud of your accomplishment."

"All of my life I wanted to hear those words from you and the joy is unexplainable."

"Nikki let's celebrate our love and get tattoos."

"That's a wonderful idea. Let's go."

I shut my eyelids tighter to block the bright light from shining on my face.

"What the fuck? Is it morning already? Where did the night go? How did I end up naked?"

I pull the covers back trembling in fear of seeing a man next to me, "Nothing. Thank God."

My head spins and the last thing I recall was throwing back tequila shots.

I roll on my back grimacing with pain, "What the hell? Did someone stab me last night? How many drinks did I have?"

I stare at the ceiling shaking my head, "My sister is behind this."

"Nikkiiiiiiii. Come here."

She runs in with a gigantic grin on her face, "The dead has risen."

"What happened last night? Why do I have a bandage on my back?"

She winks and says, "You mean what happened this morning. The tattoo artist didn't accept walk-ins. I suggested we go to a bar to pass the time. I didn't know you would become the life of the party. People were screaming your name while you flushed drink after drink. After the bar closed, I asked if you want to go home or get fresh ink."

"What kind of tattoo did I get?"

"You are always proclaiming Team Scorpio so I designed one to appreciate."

I peel the bandages, limp to the mirror to check and recheck the extra-large scorpion drawn on my lower back with Malakai's name between the claws and the sting pointing towards my birthdate.

"Damn this tattoo is the shit. I love it."

I am in awe of the incredible muse he created for my future husband.

I pull up Nikki shirt, "What did you get?"

She slaps my hand, "None of your damn business. I'm saving my ink for Corbin eyes only."

"Whatever. Which body part is the tattoo resting on?"

She slaps her ass and make it clap, "Booty cheeks. When he eats my ass, he'll be delighted seeing himself."

"Bitch you are stupid with a super S. Give me some love."

She slides her hand around my waist and I playfully slap her face, "Don't touch Malakai."

When the tattoo heals, I will send a picture of it with more letters. I slide to my radio and play his favorite song *Closer to my Dreams* by *Goapele*.

.

Chapter 25

Malakai

I'm no Einstein but I know Necole's name is written all over it. The drama would have been acceptable if I busted her guts or milked her throat; I never touched her.

Waiting to be ambush with more foolishness, I take a few deep breaths, exhale and lift the box.

I slam my fist into it, clutch the flap and rip it revealing a card, cell phone and dress. I reach for the card with Asperilla's head cut off the picture with the words, *"LOL, Women lose their head over you"* on the front. Flip the card and instructions for me to watch the videos on the cellphone.

Shaking my head. What groupie sends an expensive *iPhone* to her secret crush?

Unlock the code, tap the app and 35 videos appear. I press the first one and a woman in a purple dress lying in bed with a fedora covering her face.

The best thing about being a poet is the power of observation. Necole is thick like grits with yellow skin glowing under the light, manicured toes and purple lipstick. Within 15 seconds of watching, she pulls a *Master Series 4x Oppressor Butt Plug* with a four finger grip. She's better than *Houdini* making nine inches disappear in her asshole. She yanks it out, roll the tip over her clit and insert it back. She assaults herself with forcibly thrust, jabbing deeper and deeper.

The second time the plug flowed out I knew the journey. She stretched her mouth, tickled her lips and swallowed leaving the grip displayed.

The phone slips from my hand and drops to the floor. Damn this bitch is sexy as fuck.

I clutch the bulge and speak to my dick, "Simmer down young man, this kind of pussy is dangerous."

She has my attention in many ways. I'm praying I don't kill her since someone can benefit from her skills.

I scramble again through the box and retrieve the dress identical to the one in the video. This dress looks familiar. Replaying images in my head then the Latino chick pops up. Gotcha! I knew I saw this dress before. I race to the computer, type my name on *YouTube* and find the chick I ejaculated on at the club. None of this shit makes sense. How did Necole get the dress? It is becoming creepier with every gift I receive from this erotic lunatic.

Fuck this. Undercover Brothers owe me an update.

I run into my study room to call them on the secure line.

Someone answers after the third ring, "Undercover Brother, we track deep in the sheets so you can sleep in peace."

"Man, didn't I tell you last time to change your slogan."

"Fuck you Malakai."

"Where do we stand with my situation? Any leads?"

"It helped more if you gave a last name but no worries. The postal worker provided information once money was shown. We know where she lives however you should speak to Dr. Russell at the *Central Florida Behavior Hospital* before you approach her."

"I guess that explains her psychotic behavior. Thanks for everything and the money will be wired to your account."

"You need to wire some pussy before you get out the game."

"I gotcha next time."

We clear the call and I'm a little closer finding who the hell is Necole.

I place my head on the desk to clear my thoughts. I'm pissed because I am going to a Whore Rehab, being faithful and trouble is at my front door.

"Love Divine it would be nice to see your face. I know you would have the perfect solution to correct my nonsense. If you are listening, nudge God on the arm because I really hate to kill this bitch for being obsessed through my poetry. My wedding is coming and dealing with this shit. Asperilla is on cloud nine, floating around singing songs and fucking my brains out. I want the best for her, hell I want the best for my damn self. I'm unsure how long I can maintain this secret."

"Not long enough you fucking bastard."

Raising my head from the desk; Asperilla holds the dress and phone.

I smack my forehead. Shit! I left it in the room when I needed to use the phone.

I mumble, "Fuck me," under my breath. Could this day get any worse?

"Asperilla I can explain."

"You can't explain a damn thang. We agreed to be one and you are deceiving me."

I wish I can swallow a red pill to bring me out of this. Unfortunately, it only existed in the *Matrix*.

I stare at my feet refusing to make eye contact. My next words will either save the wedding or she'll put a bullet between my eyes.

"Asperilla please, I will tell you everything."

She places her hands on her hip. "I'm waiting."

"Umm did you watch the video?"

She slings the phone and bounces off my chest, "Yea idiot."

It's a blessing she didn't hit my face but my chest burns. When Asperilla is pissed only two things calm her, fear and dick. Neither will work if she wants to slice my balls and place them in a mason jar.

I leap out the chair, grab her swiftly and pin her to the sofa, "Asperilla don't throw shit at me again. Let me explain."

Her facial expression become less tense as I tell her everything from the beginning until now.

She let out a sigh, "You are heavy and pressing on the baby."

I jump and step towards the book shelf, "What did you say?"

"I'm pregnant, I think it happened when you scaled the walls and fucked me out the window."

I reach for her hand and gaze in her eyes, "When were you going to tell me?"

She snatches her hand, "At the damn eulogy and that's what you get for fucking slut bucket bitches."

"Asperilla I thought we had an understanding about my demented groupie."

"I'm fucking with you Malakai. You could have told me sooner."

"I didn't want to deprive your happiness. You have been looking forward to your wedding day since I proposed. We survived worse and I'm tackling this one myself."

She rubs my shoulder, "Malakai we are a team; two bullets are better than one."

"You mean heads."

"Nah I mean bullets. My pistol thinks for itself."

Pressing my face against her stomach, "If it's a boy, we are naming him *Makaveli*."

Pushing my face away, "Get the fuck out of here. I'm praying for a girl."

"Who would have imagined a fucked up day could create an incredible surprise?"

I bit her earlobes, open her blouse, unlatch the bra and sensually lick her areole. Soft chews on the tip, engulfing one by one and releasing cool air until they reach the fullest peak.

She gasps between kisses and tonight we are reliving the power of creation.

Chapter 26

Malakai

I wasn't expecting this type of visual when I arrive to my destination. I pictured an asylum filled with *Hannibal Lector* face masks and strait jackets. This hospital is the opposite of any movie I have seen; neatly trimmed hedges, clean sidewalks and colorful painted exterior.

I scroll to the front desk, "Hi, my name is Mr. Malakai and here to see Dr. Russell."

The receptionist stays buried in the computer striking keys like lighting hit her hands.

She tilts her glasses, "Please have a seat and Dr. Russell will be with you in a minute."

The waiting room is peaceful and a *Jet* magazine sits on the coffee table. I flip to the beauty of the week and memorize her measurement.

"Malakai I presume."

Shaking his hand, "Good Morning Dr. Russell."

"I'm glad you came. We have some vital things to discuss. I apologize for not revealing it over the phone."

He escorts me down the hall to Necole's old room. My first step inside reminds me of *The Twilight Zone.* There are army duffle bags, pictures plastered against the wall and copies of my spoken words CDs and DVDs on her nightstand.

Dr. Russell clears his throat, "Have a seat and I will clarify a few things. Necole came to us two years ago after witnessing the death of her husband during a carjacking."

"The police found her covered in blood and eating brain fragments. Some people thought she was involved with his death but couldn't prove it. The state found her not guilty and recommended mental rehabilitation. Her first week created the worst turmoil my staff ever experience from a new patience. She wouldn't eat, sleep nor speak. She chewed a nurse's nose, drank her own urine, defecated and played in it like *Play-doh*. Her behavior drastically improved the third week. She snatched the custodian's phone when it rung with a tone of your poetry. Every time she heard your voice, she changed from a psychotic state to normal. The medical team video recorded her process and couldn't understand the calmness she became. She ate, socialize with patients and after 6 months a success story for modern science. With all the medication in the world, it was music, your music that healed her wounded heart."

I rip my picture from the wall, "Fuck science! I need answers on how to deal with this chick."

He hands me the report, "I dug deeper into her case after your friends contacted me. I didn't know about her troublesome childhood until my colleague from *California* faxed her records."

I shuffle through the papers and discover something that causes the hair on my neck to stand.

Her real name is Necolette Robinson and at the age of 5 was diagnosed with schizophrenia.

I cannot believe the shit I'm reading.

Patient is known to transform into a Nikki character and carries a conversation with herself. This person will protect her from danger or command her thoughts and actions. Prescribe antipsychotics medication to stop future breakdowns.

The report states she was normal all the way into her twenties with no recurrence of symptoms.

"Dr. Russell how could you accept a patient and not review her past medical evaluations?"

The sparkle from his ring finger tells the answers.

"No response. Money rules the medical field as well as pussy."

There is an updated photo in the file and her features are remarkable. It's unbelievable how a woman can be beautiful and a basket case at the same time.

"Malakai don't quote me, Necole thinks you're her husband. She is a walking time bomb without her meds; no one is safe and will eliminate everything to have you."

I slide the chair back and wipe the dust off my pants, "Dr. Russell thank you for enlightening me."

I rush out before he says anything. Seventy-five percent of this could have been solved if a thorough follow up was conducted. Now I truly understand why the life of a whore is dangerous.

I dread leaving with this information but the drive to *Tampa* gives me time to think. I reach in my glove department, pull the first letter and replay her words. *Malakai, we have met before and I will leave you more clues later.*

What clues are you talking about Necole and why are you fucking with me?

You keep saying I enjoy teasing ladies when I perform and now the shoe is on the other foot.

I tap my fingers across the steering wheel, turn up the music and fade in my thoughts. I put her picture on the dash and study it down *I-10*.

Monique name flashes across the radio as an incoming call.

"Good Afternoon Ms. Ravishing."

"Yes that's me and don't forget it. Please stop by the club and sign the papers for next week's show."

"I'm ten minutes out. I've been preoccupied with the wedding and my serial stalker, it slipped my mind."

"Monique I need to ask a question. Say you love my work and you're my number one fan. What would make you happy and pissed at the same time?"

"Honestly it's the way you seduce women on stage. You come half naked, pulling your dick out, pack your shit and head home. Leaving them to fuck an average Joe."

My mind ran back to the show I tossed a woman, played in her pussy on stage and didn't know her name. How many have I brought to the tip of climax and left them missing ecstasy.

Shit! I slam on my break and nearly rear end the car in front. The blast from my past is over and I know exactly my next move.

"I'm parking the car; please pull my performances from the past 5 years. It looks like I'll spend the night at the club and conduct my own *WatchNight*."

I jump a few stairs, sign papers and rush to my office to watch my rawness.

Necole picture rest on my planner. Between each set, I pause to compare the woman in the video to her picture. I'm zero for 20 but I know she's in one.

Damn I fucked my pussy pocket on stage. What the hell goes through my mind?

I turn to the mini bar and mix something to calm my nerves.

For a second I hear Asperilla's voice. She never speaks during my performances. My head jerks around and Asperilla is autographing a CD. I can't make out the woman from the angle she is sitting. I grab the remote, hit rewind and it is Necole in the chair.

You love to tease ladies but now it's my turn.

Damn! I helped fuel the monster burning inside of her.

I adjust the volume and the words, "Are you ready to suck my mic, spit, suck on it and experience the explosion in your mouth."

She smiles as I glide the mic down her body over and over again; tittie fucking and rubbing under her dress.

I would have fucked her if I didn't believe in Artistic Law 101. *Never fuck fans who supports your gift.* I fast forward where Asperilla is in the scene.

I rewind back and Necole is talking to me until Asperilla walks up and kisses me in front of her.

Why is Asperilla signing that CD?

Oh Shit!

I pause to study Necole's body language. Grab my earbuds to listen deeper since her lips moved.

I tune everything out except her words.

A silent but clear whisper spoke, "Don't worry Necole. I will get you Malakai or die trying."

She had a stone cold look in her eyes and seemed possessed. Chills run down my spine after hearing the voice of my controlling psychotic stalker.

Chapter 27

Malakai

I am infamous for delivering eargasms at my performances. Going through the videos brought back extraterrestrial times of space age escapades. My erotic poetry is X-rated spitting, hot lava in their mind, blowing words against their neck and wetting panties.

I love my life as a poet and my supporters are beyond loyal. The stage is my second home and I'm not giving it up for a deranged groupie.

It's always the sexy ones who are the craziest. Hell I'm upset she's a beast with a butt plug and I can't fuck her. In another life she could have gotten me with her anal techniques.

I need to get things clear and gain what I need from Joselyn. She should close her curtains; I can see in her house from the car. I scratch my head and ponder should I be here. I didn't tell her to auction the dress or flash it on social media.

I check my clip, creep to the front door and whisper, "Please no trouble tonight. I don't want to unload shells in a jealous boyfriend."

Two soft knocks and the door opens. My thoughts to myself, *"Bitch you don't check the peep hole. No wonder Necole snuck you."*

She stands in a trance, eyes and mouth wide open. "Are you going to let me in?"

"I can't believe Malakai is at my house. My friends will never believe this."

Her lips ramble back and forth and still hasn't invited me in. I clear my throat to get her attention.

"Forgive me, where is my manners? Please come in and have a seat?"

Her home smells nice, cozy ambience but I'm not here for the scent.

"Joselyn?"

She tucks her foot under her butt and moans, "Yes."

I slide the picture and ask, "When was the last time you saw her?"

Her lips tremble and stutter, "I haven't."

"She's not coming back to hurt you. No need to be afraid. How did she get the dress?"

She takes a long pause, shifts her hair to the side and responds, "Look at my head. It was almost two months ago when I needed 38 stitches from a baseball bat; doctors said I could have been brain dead."

My eyes shift to the ceiling thinking this bitch is a drama queen and the scar is barely visible.

"I didn't come to give sympathy dick; let me correct my wrong and leave."

I reach in my pocket and hand her the money attached to the clip, "This should be enough to cover your medical expenses."

Emotion on her face shifts from "damsel in distress to oh shit me and my girls are shopping tomorrow."

"Ok Joselyn, I need to know what happened when she stole the dress."

She takes a deep breath and blurts, "The bitch is a lunatic demanding I give her the dress. I slammed the door in her face and rejoined my friends. Five minutes later she returned. I was ready to punch her in the mouth but didn't see the bat swinging. Next thing, we were tied up and she ransacked my room. She told me if I wanted to live, don't call the police. Malakai why do you care?"

"I have the dress and wanted to ensure you were alive."

She claps her hands and asks, "Can I have it back?"

"It's at the drycleaners."

"Damn I had females all over interested in buying it."

She counts the money and shouts, "This is over $5,000; I'll give it back if you do something for me."

I chuckle knowing three months ago I beat my dick watching her in the club.

"What's so funny Malakai? I don't want to fuck but wondering about recreating another masterpiece."

I raise my eyebrows at her comments. Here I am in the mist of getting married, a crazy groupie and contemplating another adventure.

"Fuck it. You only live once. I want half the money you make and I'm not beating my dick with you in the dress; I'll go in the bathroom."

She runs to her room and returns with a nude silver iridescent embellished padded dress. My dick peeps the sleeveless round neck line and V-shape back.

I snatch the dress, speed to the bathroom and pull out my phone. Swipe my finger down my tongue, press play, *Lord knows* by Drake displays. Umm, not this title-skip.

I swipe my phone again and *Classic Man* comes on.
This is perfect since I only need two minutes. Swaying my
hips to the beat and unzipping my pants. Flick my tongue in
the mirror and pull my shirt to my ribcage. I unleash the
dragon, spit in my hand, shake it like dice and wipe my
dick. Fuck going slow, my strokes are swift and hard.
Jerking up, down and massaging the mushroom head.

I bit down on my lips and fantasize of Joselyn dancing
in the club. She claps her ass and I twist my arm to work
my triceps and forearms.

Bitch you want a master piece. Huh Bitch. I'm going to
shoot this nut on the dress, mirror, sink and the floor. This
hoe will need a mop to clean up this shit. One dose of
heavy cream coming up.

This shit feels good. My nut ascends and biceps flop
back and forth from impact. I squeeze my abs and close my
eyes, "Oh Fuck, come to Daddy."

My breathing intense and clench my fist tighter around
my shaft. Slam into my pelvic and last thrust comes with
explosion. The impact is similar to a Holmes kick to
Rousey head. I spray my seeds as requested.

Shit! That's one hell of a ride. Who the hell beat their
dick in a bitch's house without getting pussy? Malakai
that's who.

I watch the last drip string from my head. I play in it
then wipe some on my tongue and lick my lips; taste like
pineapples.

I clean up, adjust my pants and back to reality.

I wink and toss the dress, "Here you go baby."

She sniffs it and responds, "Smells better than the last
one."

She springs in my arms and kiss my cheek, "Thank you so much Malakai. I have a ton of freaky friends with fetishes. I'll pay you when the dress is sold."

"Thanks for affording me the opportunity to use your bathroom and stay out of trouble."

She waves the money, "Aren't you forgetting something?"

"You can use it to buy new clothes. The hustle sounds good and can easily triple our funds."

Strolling to my car thinking of artists to masturbate on dresses and suits. A crazy but profitable idea besides the money could be saved for the baby's college fund. Tonight wasn't a bad one. I checked on Joselyn, nutted on her dress and no penetration.

Turning on my car and *Classic Man* plays on the radio, how ironic is that. I'll do my remix on the way home.

"And I don't live by the law, mummafucker
I burn through pussy like whoa
When everybody's feeling so cold
I'm masturbating on Joselyn flo
And bitches get a bit of my glow
I got a tongue to get you sprung, mummafucker
Necole you are fucking with the wrong mummafucker
Treat me like a don, mummafucker"

Flenardo

Chapter 28

Asperilla

Finalizing a wedding is worse than managing a stable of wet pussy. Nervousness never played a part in my world but right now I need a good fuck.

Check the time on my *iPad*, "Where the hell is Malakai?"

I rub my belly and smile, "In three months, a cute baby bump appears."

A year ago kids were out the question. I survived a tragic childhood and my baby won't have to steal food to eat or kill a man to protect her mother. Life was rough but I'm thankful for my rags to riches story.

The video camera beeps teleporting me from my past. Malakai is at the gate. He deserves a good cussing along with an incredible fuck.

"Babe, I'm home."

I attempt to play mad as he enters the bedroom but he knows I'm happy to see him.

Throwing a pillow, "Bout time."

He yawns and says, "Today was long as hell but I found out some wild shit. My groupie is a psychopath believing I'm her Boaz. To make a long story short; she came to a show and experienced poetic magic. The doctor thinks I'm the reason behind her madness."

"It could be true. You have fucked a lot of bitches and left them with broken hearts."

He kisses my lips and says, "I'm glad you stayed."

I rub my fingers demonstrating the *Manziel* money gesture, "It's all about the dinero."

"What are you doing about your stalker?"

He tosses the picture on the bed, strips out of his clothes and replies, "Here ya go."

"Malakai you won't believe this shit but I know her."

"Yea from the club."

"Fuck that. I bought that broke hoe a wedding dress two weeks ago."

His serious face changes and laughs at my statement. "You did what? That's the funniest shit I heard all day."

He sits on the bed and massages my shoulders, "Baby it's alright, we'll get it back."

I mush his face, "Fucka I don't want the dress except to bury her in it."

"Sit your pregnant ass down. We can get passed these issues without taking her life. I'll make sure she returns to the hospital."

"I should choke you for saying crazy shit. Please put a bullet between her eyes and be done with it. What's stopping you?"

"She loves my poetry, maybe too much. I'm not comfortable with killing a fan."

"Back in the day you told me to fix problems now swallow your advice. I trust you but if my wedding is ruined; I'm killing you and her. Take a shower so we can fuck."

He springs up, salutes and says, "Aye aye Captain."

He shakes his ass imitating a stripper and flapping his dick between his thighs. Malakai butt sits like *Leonardo da Vinci* sculptured it. Prison is no place for him; he'll fight every day.

I sling my clothes to the floor, spread my legs, and roll sticky saliva on my clit; squeeze my nipples and rock from pleasure. Slide a finger to my ass crack, easing up slow, and finger fuck my pussy. Two more filling my wet hole gyrating my hips to match the rhythm; pull them out and suck one by one. Taking my time licking my juices, switching hands and repeating. I blow spit bubbles, lean over and release a gigantic glob landing on my clit.

Running my fingers through my hair and moans, "Ooh ooh oooh," while speeding the other ones over my lips.

My legs move back and forth from the intensity. I cuff my fingers and fuck myself equivalent to four piglets' dicks stabbing my pussy at once. Close my mouth, breathing out my nose and thrusting to meet my fingers. This nut breaks through and my legs part wider.

Malakai replaces my hands, slides his nose over my lips and suffocates my clit with his mouth. He works his tongue as I suck the juices off my thumb.

"Umm, taste good Papi?"

He can't answer with a mouthful of juicy pussy. I snatch his ears, smother his face and reminisce of fucking hoes with a strap-on. He takes a beating and keeps eating.

"Oh shit. I'm cumming."

"Muthafucka, you hear me?"

"Ahh Ahh," I release my love and he drinks my well dry.

Fucking and sucking is my version of *Busch Garden*. I can ride face and throw up cum instead of food.

He dismounts from his position, chews on my bottom lip and boasts, "Did you miss me?"

"Yes baby I did and I'm feeling extra freaky. I am going to take you where erotic poetry meets Asperilla."

He has a puzzled look on his face and responds, "What are you up to?"

"Trust me baby you will love it. Recite poetry while I suck your dick."

Rolling on his back, slapping his dick and saying, "We ready."

Shaking my head knowing I'm up to evil stuff.

He flows while I twist and stretch his dick. Part my mouth, head down and slurp up. I repeat the technique to throw him off but he shoots more rhymes. Travel to his nutsack and snatch them with my teeth.

"Malakai grab the oil under my pillow."

It doesn't take long to rub the lubricant over my hands and his dick. I lower my face to his ass and swipe my tongue. Wow he didn't stop me. The first time I tried; he slapped me.

I curl the tip of my tongue and run it over his hole. My magical hands interrupt his poetry and he enjoys my service. I trail soft kisses from cheeks to shaft and fingernail tickling his ass. Gripping and jerking his meat in my mouth, I squeeze one finger in his ass, spit on his dick and suck.

Yes, he's not stopping me. I'm conquering his ass.

Sloppy head is the best but my oral episode is close to ending.

Unleashing his dick from my jaws and drift to his balls. My hand stimulates without missing a beat. I'm testing the waters circling his asshole with my fingernails. Creeping into his vault with no interruptions.

I didn't waste time increasing the strokes of the hand job and my tongue. He loves this shit and fuck what the world thinks. Real freaks love to have their dick sucked while a woman finger fucks their butt. My tongue is the best prostate tester.

He whispers, "Stroke faster."

I throw a "thumbs up" in agreement. Mouth game and hands are on one accord and the choir will sing. Wiggling my face against his cheeks, beating his dick faster and he moan cries of passion.

"Oh fuck," he screams.

I'm in full pursuit sucking his ass like peaches; saliva dripping down my face and I want him to burst.

"You ready for my blast," he said.

"Yes Papi. Bust that thick nut on your chest."

He slaps my hand away, subs in the game and pounds his dick.

"Let me see you play in your pussy. Let me see dammit."

I stand on the bed and penetrate my wetness.

"Stick all your fingers in. Don't hold back. Fuck that pussy for me!"

I love when he takes command and his dick is in a sleeper hold getting life choked out.

"Malakai please cum baby."

He sucks his stomach in and out, utter words like he's speaking in tongue.

"Watch me nut slut. I'm about to – "

He couldn't get the last word out before it spews out; thick, creamy, and beautiful. I want to drink cum off his nipples.

I spread it inside his navel, over his lips and suck some off my fingers.

"Victorious," I shout.

"Sit down somewhere, you haven't won anything."

"Bullshit! You said a woman could never tongue fuck your ass."

He laughs and responds, "No woman can however my future wife can do a lot of things."

"For real? Maybe I'll use the lipstick next time."

"Asperilla go to bed. You are going to damn far."

I peck his lips, "I love you Malakai."

"I love you too baby."

Rest my head on his chest, rub my fingers through his head and sleep inhaling our sexual scent.

Chapter 29

Necole

"Nikki the phone is ringing, answer it. I'm about to shampoo my hair."

I do as my sister suggest and take a break from stressing over Malakai. I sent my last package with the video and I know my ass plug turned him on. My hole is swollen from it but my boo is worthy of many surprises.

I lather my head and massage my scalp under the lukewarm water. I'm feeling wonderful and drift off envisioning Malakai in the shower brushing his lips across my shoulder, squeezing my cheeks and gliding his dick across my back. His hands flow to my clit, plucks my lips open, grabs my throat and fucks me from behind.

I'm gasping for air between each stroke while he pounds my insides out. He asks me to beg for his dick and I'll do anything he wants. He sinks his teeth into my shoulder like *Dracula* piercing a woman's neck. This is the perfect time for him to piss on my back; allowing warm urine to run down my legs.

I tug the strings of my hair moaning, "Go deeper Daddy, this is your pussy."

I lean over, brace my hand against the wall and bounce my ass to unify our stroke.

I'm obsess, oh shit. That's the spot. Ram your dick in my juicy budussy.

He pokes his head through my asshole similar to birth delivering backwards. His dick electrifies and my pussy pulsates with every thrust.

My head spins and not sure if I'm cumming or shitting on his dick; either way I'm making a mess.

I turn my head over my shoulder and lunges his body into me. He snatches a fist full of my hair, yanks my head back growling, "Bring that pussy here girl."

"Fuck me harder Poet."

He slams my face against the wall, pressing his forearm against me to prevent movement. Cum flows down my thighs and my asshole burns from the dickslaughter.

"Turn around and catch this nut in your mouth you fucking cunt."

I spin around, drop to my knees with my mouth open and ready for his love offering.

He slaps my face repeatedly until I gargle his delicious nut. It stings; I love it rough and do what he asks. Why is he beating me?

My eyes blink open and a hand strikes again, "Get your crazy ass out the shower. I've been calling your name for the longest. Did you blackout?"

I stagger to my feet, "Nikki, please don't hit me again."

"Bitch hurry the fuck up, we have a problem."

She leaves and I finish washing my hair and skin. I have no idea how long I've been in here but one thing for sure, Malaki fucked my brains out in my mind and I want the real thing.

I glance in the mirror and my face is red from her slaps. She is going to pay for this shit. I wrap my hair in a towel, slip on my robe and walk to the den.

"What is it Nikki? I was drinking my protein before you interrupted me."

"Press play on the voicemail and listen. It's our old friend."

I tap the passcode and a familiar voice echoes through the speakerphone.

"Good Morning Necolette,

This is Dr. Russell and a special friend of yours visited me last week. I was informed about your setback. I'm asking you to come to the hospital for the medical treatment you need. My number is 407-238-5689. Please give me a call at your earliest convenience."

Nikki slams her fist on the counter and screams, "I'm not going back."

She goes berserk; flipping chairs, throwing dishes and cussing. She did two years for me and now is the time I compensate her.

I clasp her arms and assure her, "Calm down. I promise you will never see that hospital or Dr. Russell."

I lead her to the sofa providing my lap as comfort to rest her emotions.

I sing our song *"Me and you, us never part. Makidada. Me and you, us have one heart. Makidada. Ain't no ocean, ain't no sea. Makidada. Keep my sister away from me.*

I rock her until she falls asleep, find my cell phone and dial Dr. Russell.

"Hello?"

"Dr. Russell this is Necole. I'm willing to meet you later this afternoon."

"Necolette where is Nikki?"

"She's sleeping and you can't have her. She has suffered enough. I'll take her place."

"I see. Necolette, I'll look forward to your return.

"One more thing Dr. Russell."

"Yes."

"Never call me Necolette again."

I end the call and contemplate how to protect my sister.

I am stranded on the side of the road with a flat tire, luckily Dr. Russell agreed to give me a lift to the hospital. I'm ready to get this shit over so my sister can enjoy her freedom. I borrowed a car from Benito since Nikki said I couldn't use hers.

Dr. Russell's car pulls behind me. He gets out and says, "I didn't think you would come this easily Necolette."

I roll my eyes and quench my face. I warned him to remove my name from his vocabulary.

"This is a simple fix; I'll grab your spare tire and jack."

He walks to the rear, rummages through the trunk and asks, "Where's your lug wrench?"

"Behind you," I yell.

I raise the wrench behind my head and strike the first blow. Blood gushes from his head and he attempts a defensive stand. He turns around and I deliver a hit to his face knocking out his teeth and his body slumps to the ground.

"Please Necolette, you don't have to do this. I'll never bother you again. Your secret is safe with me."

Staring at a pathetic shell of a man begging for his life and I feel no sympathy only rage. I whack him again for saying my name and the wrench caves into his forehead.

My adrenaline is high and I don't remember lifting him until the trunk wouldn't close.

Damn, his leg is hanging out.

I flip it over, step back to appreciate my work and slam the trunk.

My second kill has increased my gutty side. My fingers weren't trembling, heartbeat is normal and I'm totally calm. After the body is disposed, I'm going home, take a bubble bath, masturbate and spend the evening with Malakai's pictures.

I call *Trademark Metals Recycling* and order, "Hurry and pick up this car."

Within twenty minutes a truck pulls in front and grabs the car.

I throw the keys and ask, "What about the other car?"

I shrug my shoulders, "Make a second trip and take it."

Dr. Russell's car won't make it to the scrapyard. The driver looks like an idiot and will probably joyride. It's not everyday someone ask to scrap a *LS 460*.

"Do you need a ride ma'am?"

"Yes, I'm riding to watch you smash it."

About thirty minutes later, I see the scrap yard on my left.

I mention to the driver, "I'll pay extra if you demolish my car first."

The glean in his eyes brighten and responds, "No problem ma'am."

He hops out the truck, unhooks the car and whistles for a coworker to assist him.

He asks, "Could you give me an hour to remove the engine and other parts to resale?"

I cross my arms, "Sure but don't take all day."

They dismantle swiftly; beating and pulling parts from everywhere. When he finished, he whistles, "Johnny bring the crane over here."

The claws hover the car, swoops down to pick it up and releases into the bale.

The driver states, "Step back for your safety."

I respond, "I want to watch you crush it all. I'll be fine."

"Whatever floats your boat ma'am."

He presses the button and the steel metal lowers squashing the vehicle in slow motion. I step around to see the finish product.

Here lies the car and Dr. Russell in a square shaped bale of metal. You would have thought I received a master's degree the way I am jumping up and down screaming, "Yes."

Justice is gruesome but my sister is safe.

Chapter 30

Nikki

"Corbin your invitation of moving in together is overwhelming. Why are you being generous to a woman you barely know? Why aren't you married? You are a handsome, wealthy man and I'm sure women flops at the sight of your presence."

He kisses my hand and responds, "You didn't."

My heart flutters whenever he pecks my knuckles. He promises tonight will be an extraordinary date with a breakfast in bed finale.

The way the word bed escapes his lips causes my pussy to quiver from the image penetrating my holes. I can't wait to lick his cum and suck the skin off his dick.

I throw the thoughts away, hug Corbin's neck and ask, "Where are we going?"

"Wouldn't you like to know and telling will ruin the surprise."

I go along with his plans, letting him control the activities. We enjoy a smooth ride to our unknown destination. The car halts and the driver taps the window.

Corbin rolls down the window and the cool breeze blows through the car. I cover my braless chest from exposing my harden nipples.

He winks his eye and kisses my cheeks, "I'll be right back."

He travels around to open my door displaying endless charm. My love grows deeper every minute I'm around him.

He extends his hand, helping me to my feet and points toward a helicopter, "You are my angel and tonight I'm taking you back to heaven."

"Where is the pilot?"

"You are staring into his eyes. Are you afraid?"

"I fear nothing when I'm with you."

We ascend into the skies catching a bird's eye view of *Davis Island Homes* of the rich and famous.

"Below us is the *Palace of Florence Apartments*. Its architectural structure is a mixture of medieval and classical elements. It includes a four-story battlement tower."

Corbin continues speaking about the building and I am mesmerized by the knowledge and history flowing out of him.

We fly downtown, past *Bayshore Boulevard* traffic and over the *Port of Tampa*.

"Do you love dolphins?"

"I haven't seen any but they are cute on TV."

He chuckles at my statement and I am embarrassed for saying it.

"No worries, a lot of people stay here and never noticed them."

He sweeps over *Hillsborough Bay*. I am not afraid but being in a helicopter over water is not my cup of tea.

"You can open your eyes and peep," he insists.

The magical scene is out of a movie. The dolphins frolicking in the water having the time of their lives. I can't ask for anything else in a man. His desires to have me and the next time he inquires; I am saying yes.

We return safely to the airport and he asks, "Did you enjoy your trip to heaven?"

I couldn't answer from blushing. He doesn't mind pouring compliments over me. He notices the color of my makeup, sizes of my clothes and exotic scents of my perfume. He is the complete package and that's scary; everything perfect comes with skeletons.

Driver asks, "Where to Mr. Corbin."

"Home my friend. Take us home."

We travel to the house less than ten minutes away. My eyes jump out of my head pulling into the driveway. Corbin is holding out on me. I leap out to touch the front door to make sure I wasn't dreaming.

Taping his shoulder, "Your house is flamboyant as your lifestyle. Why didn't you tell me you live on the island?"

"I don't."

My feelings are similar to a punch in the chest and struggling to breathe. If my eyes could shed tears of sadness; he would recognize them.

He smiles and announces, "Nikki the house is yours. I bought it the other day when you mentioned you need time from your sister."

The only words I can muster is, "I love you."

He kisses my earlobe and says, "What are you waiting on. Go in."

The floor covered in Brazilian walnut wood and he announces again, "Look up."

He says, "The ceiling was hand painted by a Moroccan artist in Casablanca. To the left and right are spiral staircases leading upstairs."

I'll check the kitchen later; jot upstairs, fall in love with the master bedroom and the custom walk in closet. I reach my hand back to feel Corbin's but he wasn't there.

Damn, I left him downstairs in the mist of excitement.

I'm making a fool of myself. I lower my head and take slow steps to rejoin him.

"It's okay baby I'm still here."

I lift my head to the sound of his voice and he's naked, erect, chiseled chest, tight abs, with a pink rose in his hand. Is he Superman? Everything he does is out of this world?

He places the rose in his mouth and mumbles, "Follow me."

I assume upstairs however he leads me to the patio. The only light comes from a fire pit; cozy and romantic atmosphere with wine, dessert, and fruit.

He glides toward the chaise lounge daybed, pat his hands and says, "Make yourself comfortable."

How can I get comfortable when he's stroking the hardest dick I have ever seen?

Fuck being ladylike, I pour wine and guzzle it. I grab the whip cream, shake the can and cover his dick.

"Where's the cherry," He asks?

I retrieve it with my teeth, drops it in his mouth and instruct him to chew it. I pull the dress over my head, unhook my bra, slide my underwear off and keep my heels on.

I straddle my pussy over his face, stretch wide and slurp the whip cream. He pumps his dick in my mouth and I slide my hands under his thighs to gain the advantage. He slaps my cheeks and sweeps his tongue through me.

We're moaning together and sucking goes full throttle throating him down and up. He turns me sideways and fingers my pussy as I suck the last trace of cream.

My juices splash on the daybed and my throat itches for his seeds. He lifts my body and reverse sixty-nine with his dick in my face. He arches a few inches off my chest, pumps his dick in my mouth ferociously and continues to finger fuck me. This angle is lovely and his balls smack my nose. Spreading my legs farther apart to reach my G-spot.

He burrows deeper, licking my slit simultaneously, slurps become louder as he increases the momentum of his thrusts.

He sings, "I love your throat."

He jerks a few times and the taste of triumphant cum soothes my mouth and swallowing every drop. His head falls between my legs from exhaustion.

After a few minutes, he jumps and asks, "Do you want to see the dolphin again?"

"What the hell?"

I'm not going back into the helicopter until he forces his dick in me.

He grabs my ass, lifts me, leaves my shoulder and head resting on the bed. He enters slowly with divine strokes and smiles.

"This is the dolphin I am referring to, now fuck me."

The position is too kinky for me but I'm willing to try anything. He teases me; ramming inches in and pulling everything out except the head.

"Corbin, fuck the common sense out of me."

He strokes and asks, "Are you sure you want that."

"Yes baby fuck me."

He releases the position and throws my legs over his shoulder. Drops to his knees and jabs it rough like I command.

"Harder baby. Fuck me harder."

He breaches unknown territories spreading my legs eagle style and my only goal is to cum.

"Ohh Ohh Ohh, yes that's it baby. Fuck this pussy."

I caress my clit as he bangs; repositioning my legs and resting my knees against his chest. He grabs my head and ravages his dick through my hole. I'm sweating, he's sweating but neither wants to stop.

"Eat my pussy, suck on my clit now."

He pulls out, buries his face in my drench and sticky cunt. His tongue drills through my lips and I face fuck him during the sucking and pulling.

"Bite the clit Corbin."

His teeth gnawing on my meat is sensational.

"Suck it baby. Yes, suck it. Ahh. Ahh Shit."

My world of frustration ends in his mouth, "Whew. I'm glad we waited; you are marvelous with your skills. After my pussy stops throbbing, we can fuck before the morning breaks."

He pulls the blanket over our naked bodies and say, "You're my angel and if the helicopter didn't get you to heaven then the orgasm gave you wings."

Chapter 31

Nikki

"My friends, we are gathered here today to celebrate one of life's greatest moments. Giving recognition to the worthy and beauty of committed love and adding our best wishes to unite Malakai and Asperilla in holy matrimony. If anyone can show just cause as to why they may not be lawfully joined together, let them speak now or forever hold their peace," says the preacher.

"This is your time to say something; for once in your life don't be chicken shit. You can't let an undeserving bitch marry your dick. Look at that hoe prancing in her white dress like Snow White. I should have brought poisoned apples to knock her ass out. She knows damn well she's not a virgin and will never love him the way you can," Nikki speaks irritably.

"Girl be quiet; you are interrupting the ceremony besides I am looking at Malakai's irresistible body. He has the soul of a Greek God with extra trimmings; tuxedo hugs his tight ass causing my lips to stick to my thong. I need to cross my legs in the other direction to give my inferno hole some air," Necole says.

I smile at her joke and quickly answer, "Fuck their wedding. I should go and slap the veil off that bitch face."

A man places his hand on my shoulder and says, "If you keep talking, I will ask you to leave."

I'm ready to snap but I keep a ladylike composure and watch the wedding even though it sickens my stomach.

The ceremony continues, Malakai says his lovely vows and the setting is perfect. Every woman desires the same thing but he belongs to us.

I can't believe it is at the beach. The groomsmen and bridesmaids are dressed in ravishing colors. Everyone's barefoot or wearing sandals with their attire.

I envy this bitch. Maybe I should help Necole find another man. Unfortunately, no one on this planet can make love to her body and mind like him.

Asperilla recites her vows and I listen closely as she admits her life was empty before he came. He is the light to her darkness, the pulse to her heartbeat and the father of her child. I hear the last statement and ready to act a fool. Necole tries to hold my crazy ass back but it is too late.

I stand and say, "Oh hell naw, Asperilla ain't shit but a slut. There's no telling who the father of her child is. Malakai don't love you and he never will. He loves my sister Necole and she needs to know the truth."

Everyone looks our way and I don't give a damn of the scene I create.

I say louder, "We are not leaving until Necole gets her man."

"Get your fucking hands off me," I shout, as people grab and escort me out; I am not leaving without confrontation.

A female voice yells, "Let her go."

I see Asperilla running and I am ready for a fight. I look for Necole and her scary ass ran off. I will deal with her later.

They let me go and Malakai comes to stop us. A smile on my face as the knight in shiny armor runs to rescue a damsel in distress. My happiness comes to a halt when Asperilla steals the first punch and I fall backwards. I lose my balance and hit the sand.

She stomps me with her bare foot and before she gets to my face, Malakai grabs Asperilla and says, "Stop! Your ass is pregnant."

He looks at me and say, "I don't know you or want your ass. You better leave before a body bag takes you home."

I know he is upset. I reach for him and immediately feel a sharp pain between my fingers. Blood pours down and I am going into shock seeing my finger hanging by its meat. This day can't get any worse. I'll die first before I let these fuckers enjoy their happiness.

I scream as they evict me off the beach, "Malakai and Necole foreverrrrrr!"

"Nikki wake up! Wake up! You are having a bad dream."

I jump from a startled touch and fall on the patio floor checking my hands for blood.

"Are you ok?"

I stare at Corbin's face for what seems like eternity before answering, "I believe so."

He lifts me to the daybed, run his fingers through my hair and asks, "Did the dream have something to do with Malakai."

I am flabbergasted when his name is heard.

This was something I couldn't brush off or cover up. My heartbeat racing like taking the hardest test in my life and time is running out.

I sigh and ask, "How did you know?"

He secures me, kisses my forehead and answers, "You called out his name last night."

"I apologize for ruining the beautiful sunrise we should be sharing. There is so much to say but not enough time."

"Try me. I'm different from most men. I'm assuming he's more than a friend since you have scorpion ink with his name. I noticed the tattoo after licking your back to your ass cheeks; by the way I love my face on your butt."

"What the fuck!"

I break his hold, run in the house and find the nearest mirror. The design for Necole rests on my back. How the hell did it get there?

I snatch the vase from the table, throw it in the mirror and watch it shatter into pieces.

"That's not my tattoo," I scream.

My mind is all over the place and the dream was a wakeup call. I have to find my sister and deliver her Malakai.

Corbin comes in and says, "It's going to be alright. I can help you."

"I don't need your help. I need to be at home protecting my sister."

He grabs my hand, attempt to kiss my knuckles but I pull back.

"I'm not in the romantic mood right now. The fuck was good; you have a beautiful heart however I'm not the woman for you. You should find someone else."

"I don't want another woman. I deserve you. Faith brought us together."

"Look at me dammit. I'm an emotional wreck. Tell your driver to take me home now."

"Stay with me; my people will work with you. My mom was schizophrenic and my dad patience wore thin caring for her. The signs were written on your face from the moment you talked to yourself at the restaurant. You reminded me of her and I don't want to lose you."

"If you don't get the fuck outta my face with that bullshit ass story. There is nothing wrong with me."

"Are you calling me crazy too?"

"Let me clear the air. I served two years in a mental hospital for killing my sister's husband. Don't judge me. Never judge me. You have no idea the type of shit I went through to become the woman I am. Please ask your driver to take me home before I do something I might regret."

"Nikki, don't go. I'll accept your flaws and all."

He drops to his knees, kiss my toes and begs me to stay.

Damn he has won me over again.

I open my leg and his tongue rides into a pool of moisture. I grip my hair as he eats the pain away.

I love Corbin and I'll return after I help Necole. One day he will understand the love for my sister is thicker than dick and money.

Chapter 32

Malakai

For the last two weeks I have tried calling Dr. Russell for an update on Necole. I'll try a final time before things are done my way.

I throw the phone to the dashboard. Shit, another damn voicemail.

His family has filed a missing person report but I've been in the game long enough to know he's dead. The last thing he said was I think I can bring her back to the hospital with no trouble.

I warned him about her mental state and how she flips personalities. He attempted to put me in my place by saying he's the doctor and I'm the poet. I guess they will place the message on his obituary because he's never coming home. I shake my head in disgust and wonder why people are so damn hardheaded.

I watch Necole apartment complex from my window; quiet neighborhood, perfect place to raise kids and everyone mind their business.

After following her around last week, it's amazing how she lives a normal lifestyle and transforms into a psychotic werewolf; maybe she has a full moon on her watch.

I followed her to *Aldo* one evening. She held a full conversation asking Nikki did she think I would wear *Godefroid* boots.

The shocking part was the response. She said, "Fuck him; he ought to be glad we thought of his punk ass."

People were pointing and staring but never asked if she was ok. The cashier took her money like any regular customer shopping.

I break from my daydream, screw the silencer on my *9mm* and journey to her front door. I am thankful the manager is a fan. I spat some poetry, signed her titties and she gave me a key with no questions.

It's time to be the greatest present she has ever received.

I turn the key and creep into the house. Wow she's a clean freak. Everything is organized and displayed like an open house. I peep the bizarre pictures on the walls. She is a Photoshop wizard, most of the photos have different clothes, makeup and hairstyles creating an identical twin illusion.

I place the picture on the shelf, tip to one of the bedrooms and discover I am the main attraction; my pictures plastered across the room like she is deep into voodoo.

How the hell you order a *fathead* image of me, Damn, I don't have a life-size three dimensional pose at my house. She cropped Asperilla pictures and replaced it with her face.

I recognized my poem titles designed in her custom made pajamas, valentine cards with my name from 2005 and my first tour schedule. Damn this bitch is crazier than *Yolanda Saldívar*.

I check my time and it's close to her coming home from Zumba in ten minutes. I'll wait in the den and watch highlights of my sorry ass *Lakers* on *SportsCenter*.

Observing the *Black Mamaba*, 6 for 25 is crazy but my antenna goes up when I hear the keys jiggle through the locks. The door opens, I turn my head and wave her in.

"Welcome home dear, how was your day?"

She drops her groceries; apples and oranges roll across the floor along with the milk.

She gives a deer in the headlight stare. I guess I will break the ice since she is speechless.

"Good Morning ummmm."

Hell I'm not sure which one I'm talking to. I'm assuming it's Nikki because Necole would have jumped on my dick.

I direct my attention back to the TV, flips a few channels and directs, "Go and clean up your mess before I mix your blood in it. We have a lot of things to discuss and you will listen."

She cleans up, put away the groceries and asks, "Would you care for a sandwich?"

I leans my head back on the sofa, throw my hands up since I am in disbelief of the shit I'm hearing. I'm just as crazy as she and respond, "Turkey on wheat with spicy mustard if you have it."

She fixes the sandwich, eases over and hands the plate. "Here you go."

She could have sprinkled rat poison on the meat. No worries, Necole would kill her if anything happened to me.

I take my first bite, "Damn girl, you make a mean ass sandwich."

I continue munching and she asks, "Why are you in my house? How did you get in?"

I wipe my mouth and flip the keys between her legs, "I won't be needing these anymore. You and your sister are really-."

This woman has me speaking like it's two of them. What the fuck. Oh well, I guess there's no turning back. "Nikki, relay this message to Necole and don't leave out one word. Tell her, I admire her ambition but the dress, letters and threats of killing my finance are too extreme for me."

"My sister is in love with you. I wanted your money at first but I have someone to give me everything I need. Once you two get married, I'm out the equation."

I shake my head, "How the fuck you get out the hospital? Where's Dr. Russell?"

"I haven't heard from him since he called last week. Necole met him and I didn't ask anything about it. I'll admit you startled me when I came in but I'm not afraid of your ass. The sandwich was a goodwill gesture to feed my future brother in law."

This woman has no idea she is the same person. I understand why the doctor asked me not to kill her. Let me try a different approach.

"Where is Necole?"

"She's running errands. I'll tell her you stopped by."

"I'm done being amused with your personalities. I'm itching to shoot a bullet between your eyes; you need help."

She shrugs her shoulders and responds, "Everyone keeps telling me that. I'm perfectly sane."

She points toward the door, "Malakai you have over stayed your welcome. Get out!"

"Who the hell are you talking too?"

She hops from the sofa, runs to the kitchen, grabs a knife and screams, "Ahhhh die muthafucka."

I side step, catch her wrist and twist until it drops.

"Let my arm go. Let me go."

"Not until you calm your ass down. You are lucky I keep a soft spot for women. If you were a man, you would have died weeks ago."

I release her arm, spin her over the sofa and on the floor. She jumps up, slaps my face and claws my shirt. I give her a quick shove. Since she's off balance, I sweep under her legs and she hits the floor.

I couldn't get to her quick enough to restrain her. She punches my nuts hard enough to drop me to my knees.

"Fuck!"

Out the corner of my eyes, she retrieves the knife and bolts toward me.

I pull my *9mm* out and click the safety off, "Take another step and death awaits you."

She keeps the knife suspended in the air before it bounces upon the floor. My nuts and ego are bruised. Getting your ass whooped by a woman doesn't sit well with me.

I grab her hair and shout, "Open your mouth."

She struggles until the silencer rest on her forehead. She opens her mouth willingly and I shove it in. "Suck on it. Suck it good."

She runs her tongue over it, slurping back and forth like a good student.

"It's a shame I have to do this for you to listen but you'll get my point."

"You and your sister have 24 hours to get the fuck out of my city and back to California. I don't want to see ya'll again."

I thump her forehead and whisper into her ear, "Necole, I know you are in there somewhere. Don't send anything else in the mail, stay the fuck away from my family or I will cut you into pieces and stuff you in a duffle bag. Do you understand the words that are coming out of my mouth or do I need to blow yours off?"

She agrees and I slowly slide the silencer.

Remember you have 24 hours and the clock is ticking. I open and slam the door leaving her the final decision.

Chapter 33

Necole

"Nikki, I'm home."

I enter the living room where she usually sips tea. There is no sign of her. The vibe is off, what's going on?

Why is a half of a sandwich on the floor? I tighten up the area, throw things in the trash and vacuum.

Why is my sister ignoring me? I accept she is in love with Corbin and hope we can go on a double date.

I head towards her room, open the door and she is throwing clothes all over. Stuffing suitcases, gym bags and trash bags; not caring which item goes in.

"What are you doing?"

She ignores my question. I shake her by the shoulder. "Snap out of it."

She turns around, wiping tears and announce, "I'm moving with Corbin. He will be here to pick me up."

I interrupt her packing and asks, "When did you make that decision."

"After your boyfriend pistol fucked my mouth. I need protection from his crazy ass. Both of ya'll are sick and deserves each other."

I drop the clothes and imagine seeing him in my living room. He was in our home. I can't believe it.

"Necole did you hear what I said. He assaulted me."

"Malakai wouldn't hurt a female. You need to stop spreading rumors about him. Maybe you offered him some pussy like the other guys I dated. You attacked him after he rejected your ass."

"I can't believe you are putting dick before sisterhood. I have no reason to lie about anything."

My nostrils flare up, tighten fist and I'm on the verge of punching this hoe in the nose if she says one more thing about him.

"Okay Necole since you are on his side. How do you explain the mess in the living room, my bleeding gums and tears that won't stop pouring? I am a tough bitch and never been afraid of a man but his smooth tormenting style is pure evil. The world thinks he's a sexy poet with words but trust me I know firsthand he's a slick ass killer. I was occupied taking out Asperilla until I miscalculated him."

"Nikki calm down, we can work this out. I'm sorry I wasn't here to protect you."

"Protect me, Bitch I'm the one always handling your situations. Bullies in school, thug ass boyfriends and let's not forget your husband who kicked your brains out. I'm fucking tired of this shit; I don't need this drama."

Her emotions are raw and I can't believe our bond is breaking over a simple fight.

"Fuck it, do whatever. I'm going to pour myself a drink."

I mix my martini uttering cuss words under my breath. She acts as if I haven't held her down at her lowest time. When she was locked up, I visited every day and gave up two years of my life waiting on her.

After my third drink I am tipsy and will pick a fight the next time she drops her bag at the door.

"Bitch where you going?"

She ignores and passes me by.

The second time she does it, I stand in the way refusing to let her to pass.

I poke my finger in her chest and asks, "Where are you going?"

She glances down, grabs my finger and sling it, "Get the fuck away from me Necole."

"I'll get out your face after you take the bags to your room. Let's talk this out; we always do."

"There is nothing to say. You took his side over mine. Corbin will protect me from everyone including your precious Malakai."

"What the hell does that means?"

"You aren't dumb; you know exactly what I'm talking about. You figure out how to get your man, I'm out."

I sip my drink and respond with something to make her stay, "I love you and I killed Dr. Russell. You don't have to go back."

She slaps my face, "You did what?"

I hold back tears and massage my cheek relieving the pain. Maybe it is the alcohol boosting my courage but I am not taking this shit.

"I did it for your ungrateful ass. You may be older but I'll beat your ass if you slap me again."

She steps aside to her room avoiding an argument and pack the rest of her belongings.

I flock on the sofa, toast a drink to myself and gulp the martini without stopping.

Fuck that bitch. If she wants to go then the choice is hers.

"Necole?"

What do she want now? Turning the volume up on the television and ignoring her for once.

"Necole, Necole, Necole? I know you hear me."

Tossing the remote and yelling, "What the hell you want."

"I'm going to take a quick shower. Please answer the door for Corbin."

"Eat my ass."

A few weeks ago I was meditating and doing positive things. Now I feel broken by my sister earth shattering news.

The doorbell rings alerting me of Prince Corbin's presence. This little prick sweeps her away on a magical carpet and expects me to stand around for it.

The bell rings again and Nikki phones goes off.

Damn he's annoying as fuck.

I run to the kitchen, grab a knife and open the door, "Ring my bell one more time and I'm slitting your throat."

"Nikki put the knife down and let me in."

"That's the problem with white men, always thinking we need help. Nikki is in the shower and I'm Necole. You are not taking her away from me, I'll kill her first."

I slam the door in his face and he is outraged. He rattles and bangs on the door.

I yank the shower curtain and realize the only person I love besides Malakai is walking out of my life. I refuse to deal with it.

I cock the knife over my head and stab the blade in her chest. Blood runs off her titties in the water. She tries to grab my hand but I plunge deeper and deeper until she slips and hit her head on the tub.

෯෯෯෯෯෯෯෯-------------------------෯෯෯෯෯෯

I open my eyes in a hospital bed. I touch my head and instead of hair, bandages are wrapped around it. My chest is tight and discover stitches under the gown.

Damn Nikki fought until her last breath. She managed to stab me. I attempt to sit up but too weak to move.

Wet lips kiss my forehead and I roll my eyes upwards. "Aww fuck, its Corbin's funky ass."

"Baby I thought I lost you. Your next door neighbor and I kicked your door in. We found you in the shower passed out. The doctor confirmed you sustained a concussion and if the knife was closer, it would have pierced your heart. I'm going to take care of you for the rest of our lives. No more pain and forget about Malakai."

I wish I had the strength to claw his eyes out for calling my baby's name. This fool has the audacity to say I can forget about him.

He kisses my knuckles and his saliva makes me nauseous.

Eww, I'll put up with this shit until I think of an escape.

Chapter 34

Necole

He is suffocating me to death. He won't leave my side for shit and I haven't had a chance to call Malakai to let him know I'm okay. I know he is pulling his hair, crying his eyes out and hopefully filed a missing person report.

I check my stitches to see how they are healing. I run my hand over my chest and my fingers scrape my heart half shape pendant. Nikki had it engraved with the words Big Sis/Little Sis. I have worn it my entire life as a symbolic bond between us.

I snatch it from my neck. Damn why you made me do it.

I throw the pendant across the room, watching it soar to the wall and landing on the floor. Life was created for new beginnings and today is my birthday.

For the past few days, I have impersonated my sister. Every time he calls her name, I take full advantage of his weakness and catch him off guard. He will serve breakfast in a few minutes. I have timed every movement and his schedule never changes.

He opens the door and brings the food to the bed.

"Hmmm, the food smells scrumptious."

I lift the tray and reveal Belgian waffles, a cucina omelet with turkey bacon. Corbin might not be as bad as I thought but he's not Malakai.

He sits and instructs me to open and chew. He slices the food and feed me similar to a small child. He kisses the leftover crumb off my lip. I reciprocate the love floating my tongue down his throat.

I relinquish the kiss and responds, "I love you and thank you for caring for me."

He twists his fingers through my hair, stares in my eyes and says, "Love makes you do things."

I finish my last bite and suggest, "Today would be perfect to go outside and feel the breeze across my skin."

I'm praying he realizes that I have been cooped up and agrees with me.

"Nikki I apologize for the hostile treatment. I take no pleasure in treating you this way. Here's your medicine and I'll check on you in a few minutes."

He pops the pills in my mouth, hands a glass of water and watches me swallow.

I open my mouth, "Ahh."

"All gone," I reply giving him the opportunity to check.

He grabs the items and exits the room; giving me time to plot my next move.

I tap my fingernail against my temple for a plan to enter my mind. Killing him could land me in jail with his law enforcement connections. When you can't think of anything else, put a dick in your mouth. I'll seduce him with the slobberknocker. This is the last time I throat a man unless it's Malakai.

I roll off the bed and scan the room for something to knock him in the head. The vase with the red roses looks like freedom. I swoop and place it closer to the nightstand.

I hop in the bed, grab my *Kindle* and read until he returns.

After twenty minutes, a courteous knock echoes the door, "What are you reading my dear?"

I wish it was *Escape from Alcatraz* but I politely respond, "*Stephen King*. You came in here for something, let the cat out."

"A week is too long to be in this room. The temperature is a nice 80 degrees, bright and sunny. The pool is ready for us to take a swim."

"Where's my bathing suit?"

He takes off his clothes and say, "Swimming naked is better. Your body is beyond incredible to be hidden."

"Thanks for the compliment."

He is fucking up my plans besides outside sounds lovely with a plan B.

I slide my boy shorts off; he unfastens my bra and bring my slippers. I follow him downstairs and this is my first time noticing his house. It is not an average district attorney salary; what type of side hustle is he involved in?

He squats and say, "Hop on my back."

Is this man always romantic? I turn my face and ask, "For what?"

He laughs and answers, "I'm carrying you to the pool."

If it makes him happy, oh well. I slide on and he wraps his arms around my legs. I thought about choking him but I am not strong enough to get it done.

I ride him to the pool; he spins around and fall backwards in the water.

I come off the water, faking my enjoyment and telling him how great the water feels.

He swims toward the edge, jumps out of the water and sits with his legs wide open. I trail him in hot pursuit, massaging his inner thighs and running my finger over his shaft. Rolling my tongue around his sac, towards the tip and flicker across his urethra. His dick doubles in size once fully erect. I suck the head slowly, caressing the ball and grabbing his dick with both hands. I twist, rub up and down; skin rising over his tip and sinking back to the base.

"I want to make love to your mouth baby. Take it all in."

I do as instructed and run my throat down until my nose bangs his pelvic. I widen my jaws for the pleasure.

He moans and groans, "Yes, let me fuck those cheeks."

I release the sloppiest slobberknocker performed, squeezing his dick and jerking my head faster. I remove my mouth, slob and precum drips from the tip like a leaking faucet. I find joy watching it hang before I slurp.

Slapping his dick over my tongue, rolling my eyes to peep his emotions. They are shut tightly, a sign of appreciation. I form a C-cup with my hands and stroke hard and fast as he begs for more.

I climb out the water, tugging nonstop on his manhood, dropping to my knees and sucking the thoughts out of his brain.

"Umm umm."

I stick my fingers inside my pussy as I bob over his dick. He grabs my head and rams it down thrusting my throat.

"Shit! Oh Shit. I love the punishment."

My fingers working overtime with juices running down my thighs. I want him to cum down my throat; hot cream explosion. The thought of the eruption makes me suck harder.

I pull my fingers out of my pussy, clamp and gobble his dick in my mouth. I repeat sucking and stroking then he pushes my head and jack his dick. I leave my mouth open while he thrusts and fist shake.

"Ahh ahh ahh fuck!"

I love that kind of music to my ears.

His ass smacks against the payment and I'm waiting to see fireworks. He yanks one last time and cum shoots like a geyser.

There he blows.

He will remember this. I run my tongue across his head and chop his dick with my teeth. Blood and leftover cum streak from the side of my mouth when I release.

He grabs his dick and screams, "Dammit."

I stand, kiss his forehead and say, "No cussing Corbin, remember you are gentleman."

I place my feet on his hip and kick him until he lands in the pool.

I throw my hand up and wave, "See you later baby."

I skip back to the house, throw on my clothes and take Corbin keys to his *BMW Z4 Roadster*.

I glance outside and notice Corbin slumped over. I couldn't leave him in a horrible predicament. I activate my Good Samaritan powers and call the maid to take him to the hospital.

As for me, I'm on a conquest to claim my poet by any means necessary.

Chapter 35

Asperilla

I've been staring at this wedding dress for fifteen minutes wondering will everything fit. My face glows whenever I rub my belly; it's a blessing I'm not showing. I would take it to a seamstress, cut out the abdominal section and have an artist paint my belly. I would vogue all the way to the altar pausing for pictures.

Malakai scent drifts in my nose and I know he is standing behind me. I spin around, leap in his arms and sink my tongue in his mouth. We rage a fight for submission, twisting each other into knots.

He eases me to the bed. I spread my legs and suggest, "Come eat your pregnant pussy."

He drops to his knees, slips a finger in my wet slit, takes it out and suck the juices.

I spread my hood on this freshly shaved pussy and say, "Talk to it before you taste it."

"What you want me to say?"

I arch my hip, glide over his nose and down his lips, "Spit some juicy poetry."

He slides his clothes off, throws my legs over his shoulder, winks his eye and say, "I have the perfect piece."

I'm a freak because I love kissing our seed and
give you all a ride to remember.
Sinking this tongue in deep,
I'll tell the embryo hello.
Back out slow, blow air on your clit, and massage your
tits.

Sending you to pure bliss with every kiss from my lips.
Blowing bubbles with your juices while you shout
harder.
Tongue dangling in and out of her third world.
Deep enough to see a cherubim standing at the Garden
of Eden while tasting your creation.

Patting my clit, "I love your thoughts; come and eat."

He opens his mouth, drools on my lips and slobs with one sweep.

This muthafucka is a sexy nasty beast. I might get my clit pierced and grant him the honor of proposing to it every night.

His mouth resembles a suction cup, gripping my pussy up in one motion. My eyes graze down and he stares back, licking and sucking my lips without blinking. He dry humps the sheets as he feasts on my lips. Watching his ass arch up and down increases my wetness. He deserves a squirt.

He drills his index finger in my pussy, bites on my clit as I play with my nipples.

"Umm Umm Umm-Oooh."

Wait a fucking minute. Why are tears rolling down my eyes? The only thing crying should be a river out my pussy.

I wrap my legs around his head and bring him deeper. He spits on my pussy, race his tongue down to my asshole and back to the clit.

"Oh Shit, do that again!"

I moan from the smacking of his lips tugging on my clit. Grabbing his head, placing one hand on top and the other one behind his neck.

"Eat this pussy like it's your last meal you fucking animal."

He growls between his licks and my pussy love the savage cry. His face was created to be fucked by me.

He hovers over my clit, fucking me faster with four fingers and I'm on the edge of losing my mind.

"Ahh Ahh Ahh. Malakai, Malakai, Malakai."

He pulls away, curves his hand inward and within seconds I gush all over. He continues to dig as the juices run down his arms and sheets.

"Aww Fuck."

I rest my heels on top of his head giving him a clear view of the explosion. He jumps face first and bathe in my pool. He speeds his fingers through my pussy like a high speed chase down the causeway. I couldn't take it anymore. The feeling vibrates my body and the squirting wouldn't stop.

"Ahh Ahh."

I kick his head accidently from the sensation, "Malakai stop!"

My pussy throbs and he continues fucking and eating knowing I'm begging for mercy. I raise my heel in the air, lunge forward and kick his forehead.

He stops, laughs and says, "You asked for it."

"Damn the sheets I purchased last week are soaked. I'm not sleeping on these."

He places them in his mouth and suck.

I slap his face, "You are a nasty muthafucka."

He comes up, kisses my lips and I feel his hardness against my thigh.

He strokes his dick and says, "Three minutes is all I need to shoot."

I know he wants it rough because I do. We can make love on our wedding day but now I want to be choked and fucked in my ass.

I flip on all fours, grab the headboard and anticipate my punishment. He tickles my lips with the head, sliding up and down while massaging my clit.

Eww, this is a wonderful feeling.

He bites my ass cheeks, unhook his teeth, slaps my ass and ask, "Are you ready?"

I bounce in the air and moan, "Fuck it right."

He mounts from behind and rocket through my pussy, "Give me this pussy bitch."

Oooh Shit, I wasn't ready. My face hits the headboard but I'll worry later, I'm enjoying the ride. I clench; tempo is hard to maintain as he pounds my pussy in a jackrabbit style. My pussy farts a tune of lust from the intensity.

My hands slip from the headboard and my face crash to the bed. Luckily it is a soft landing because he didn't give a fuck. He wants a nut and I'm his squirrel.

He presses his forearm against my lower back, pushes me in the bed and fucks harder.

"Oh Fuck!" I scream.

"Yeah bitch, I'm cumming in your pussy."

I grip the sheets for leverage and slide off his dick and say, "Not this time."

"I know you not leaving me with a hard dick. I was almost there."

I grab, squeeze his balls and place his dick in my mouth. He rocks back on his heels, thrusting down my throat and pinching my titties.

I ease his dick from my mouth, stroking him while playing in my pussy. He leans over, whisper in my ear, "Asperilla I need to cum, stop playing with me."

I beat his dick faster, "I know Papi. I stopped because I want you to cum in my ass."

His face glows from excitement and asks, "Which position?"

"Lie on your back and I'll handle the rest."

He leaks on the bed, slap his legs and says, "Hop on."

I glide my asshole over his dick and he enters like a black hole; filling to capacity. I ride slow and steady for a few minutes. Twirling my hips around as I dance on his pole.

Tossing my head over my shoulder and saying, "You love this fat anaconda."

He squints his eyes and grunts, "Yes I love your fat ass."

He plants both hands around my waist and bounce up and down like a seesaw.

"Malakai fuck me, nut in my ass and turn it into a cream pie."

My wetness increases with each thrust. Antagonizing his skills in the bedroom makes him upset.

"You can 't handle this ass. You're not man enough."

"Bitch keep talking shit; I promise you won't walk for a week."

I shrug my shoulder and my ass opens with every stroke; he will never know I'm hurting.

"Hand me the *Happiness & Joy* from under the pillow."

I turn it on and use the tip to make love to my clit. "Oh my, I'm going to squirt again."

"Fuck that pussy you dirty slut."

"Yes Papi. I love it when you call me names."

He pounds harder as I sink it in deeper.

He breathes harder, gripping nails into my thigh and holla, "Don't move."

Yes, he is about to cum but not before me. I assault my pussy between the vibrations and his dick in my ass; I'm bound to accomplish it.

I fuck myself hard, throw the toy on the floor, squeeze my clit and release.

"Asperilla I'm bout to cum."

"Cum in my ass, Cum all in my ass Papi."

I slap my clit and finger fuck my pussy as he drills the last couple of thrusts.

"Oh shit baby I love youuuuu."

The juicy nut spill through my ass; warm and thick.

"Ahh Ahh Ahh."

He screams a little more before I lift off his dick.

I explode, stand over his face and finger my pussy. I want to cum in his face again and he better not move.

"Say you love me. Say it."

He rolls his tongue over his lips and replies, "I love you Asperilla."

"Umm Umm, Malakaiiiiiiiii. Oh Shit! Aww Aww Awww."

His mouth opens as I flood his face. Juices drip from his nose and eyes. He didn't move during his baptismal.

I flop to his chest, "Whew."

I kiss the leftover juices and lay on his chest.

"Thank you for the nut," I moan.

"I should be thanking you for that gushy asshole."

"Whatever. What time is it?"

He flips the remote and the time displays 10 am.

I jump up, "Dammit, I'm going to be late."

"What the hell going on?"

I have to meet the event coordinator by noon. There is no way I can wash this cum off, do my hair and make it.

"Throw on a jogging suit."

"You crazy as hell, Asperilla Valdez rock heels and designer dresses unless I'm killing."

He slaps my ass, "Send Isabella, she isn't doing shit but eating our groceries."

"She's so quiet sometimes I forget she's here."

He points to the camera, "She's making pancakes and eggs with her hungry ass."

"Leave my damn cousin alone, she loves to eat."

I reach the door when he yells, "You can't go downstairs naked."

"She's family. She has seen titties and ass before."

He shakes his head and blurts, "Your family is beyond weird. There's no way I'll trot my ass in the kitchen with a hard dick."

I toss his shoe and hit him in the head, "Naw fucka, you like showing your dick on *YouTube*."

"Will you please stop bringing up that shit?"

"I'm only playing, relax. I'm heading downstairs; take a break because we are fucking again."

Isabella is cooking and dancing. She would have heard her name if she wasn't rocking her *beatsbydre* headphones. I sneak and wait for her to turn around.

"Holy Shit! Asperilla you scared the hell out of me."

"I tried to get your attention two minutes ago even though you rather *Salsa* in my kitchen."

"I always cook better with music. Wait a damn minute, where the fuck is your clothes?"

I tap my heels together, spin around and recite the lyrics from *Right Said Fred*.

> *I'm a model, you know what I mean*
> *And I do my little turn on the catwalk*
> *Yeah, on the catwalk*
> *On the catwalk, yeah*
> *I shake my little tush on the catwalk.*

She slaps my ass cheeks, "You play too much. Don't ooze cum in my pancake batter."

"My pussy holds cum like hostages during a bank robbery attempt."

"Get the hell out of here. What do you want Asperilla?"

"After you finish, I need you to meet with the event coordinator. I notified them that you are coming in my place. I have a proposal upstairs with the updated changes. All you have to do is hand them the packet, call me and we can conduct a conference."

She flips her pancakes and shouts, "Aww shit, I get to drive the *Jaguar* today?"

"You better return it in the same condition you found it. If I see the slightest dent or scratch, I'm whipping your ass."

"You need to take your naked ass upstairs, beat Malakai's dick and leave me alone."

"That's not a bad idea. I'll leave the envelope on the living room table and don't forget to call me when you get there."

"Thanks for doing this."

"Anytime, you know you are my favorite cousin."

"Whatever bitch. You're sucking up because you're driving my car."

"You know it. Get out of here so I can finish cooking."

Sprinting upstairs for a second serving of dick. Bust in the room, notices the empty bed and the shower running.

Snatching the door open, "Where the hell you going?"

He rinses his face, turns and explains, "Monique called and asked if I could hold a brief meeting with the staff. It seems we have a few team members unhappy with their pay."

Grabbing his dick and asking, "Can you leave this with me?"

He chuckles, kisses my lips and says, "I wish it could be with you 24/7. Do you know how much I would get accomplished if I could satisfy you at the same time?"

I slap his dick away, "Fuck you Malakai."

"I'll make it up to you later."

Inserting two fingers in my pussy then on his lips. "Open your mouth," I command.

"For what?"

"Making sure you gargle with my pussy wash."

"Asperilla get the fuck out of here so I can go."

"Damn everyone's putting me out. Fuck ya'll. I'll stay by myself."

I grab a robe from the closet and go downstairs with the proposal. Isabella meets me at the staircase holding my keys.

"Enjoy your breakfast, there's enough for you and Malakai."

I hand the envelope and she runs out the door. There's a pleasant aroma coming from the kitchen and if I have to be alone at least I won't starve.

Chapter 36

Necole

It has been a stressful week since I left Corbin clutching his royal jewels. He has a forgiven spirit. For the last two days, he has called my phone nonstop asking to speak to Nikki. I told him she's dead and to leave me the fuck alone.

Speaking of the devil, my phone rings. I slide the screen to reject, toss it out the window and pray someone runs over it. I'm delighted it was a throwaway since Malakai's pictures are in my main phone.

My life will change for the better after meeting him today. This past Wednesday I drove by his street fifty times. I would have done more if my gas light wouldn't have flashed.

I don't smoke but my nerves are getting the best of me. I bought a pack and been puffing and thumping ashes out the window all morning.

Oh my, what do we have here? Looks like Asperilla is on the move?

I know her car anywhere and doomsday comes for her funky ass. I flip the ignition and cruise a few cars behind not to appear suspicious. Her music blasts at the stoplight creating a lovely distraction for her death.

She makes a quick left towards a less crowded street. The clock reads 11:45 and my time need to happen quickly.

Fuck it. It's now or never. I speed around and bump the rear. I didn't give her a minute to slow down when I hit her ass again.

Her instinct kicks in and realizes this is not a normal collision. She accelerates, however I'm not letting her escape. I slam on the gas, aim my *P-22*, squeeze the trigger and the first bullet pierces the driver's window.

The second round shatters the glass causing the car to veer off the road, jumping the curve and crashing into a concrete wall. I place the gun down, adjust my rearview mirror and smile from the damage.

I dial Benito's number, place it on speakerphone and admits, "It's done, no more Asperilla."

"Wonderful, the club is secure for your arrival. I'll be there shortly. Keep a lookout for Malakai."

"Fuck him; I can handle his punk ass."

"Whatever. Don't fuck this up."

Tap the end button and prepare for part two of my plan. Benito wouldn't do it at first, nevertheless, flashing $50 grand and he became the right man for the job.

Since Nikki is out the way, everything in the account belongs to me. I can spurge however and whenever I please.

This car is going to the chop-shop and I am eyeing a 2016 *Jaguar*. It's the same make and model as Asperilla. It will be an early Christmas gift from Malakai.

I arrive at the club and park in his parking space. I am claiming everything in Jesus name today. I set the gun in my purse, grab my bag out the trunk and strut to the door.

Blown away from the instance I step inside. His vision is heart-stirring. This is the cure for late night boredom.

I imagine dancing on the center floor, wrapped in his arms as the crowd cheers.

I throw my head back and spin in a circle viewing the bar and DJ booth. I slow my twirls and rest my hand on my head to stop the dizziness.

Claps and praises pour in and getting louder behind me. I look over my shoulder and Benito standing with Monique; mouth duct taped but missing my sister special trademark.

I take my lipstick out and plant my image, "Monique you have been marked with the kiss of death."

Squeezing her chin, "Listen bitch, when I ask you a question, nod or shake your head. Do you understand me?"

She refuses to answer; damn Malakai has these hoes trained to be hard until the end. I'll break her one way or another.

Reach for my gun and tap it across my head, "Hmm, where can I send the first bullet? For weeks, you flaunted around my man in your sexy skirt and heels. Twisting your hips and showing cleavage every chance you get."

Grasping the trigger; bullet lodges through her thigh and blood spills down her thick lovely legs. Her eyes widen as she muffles words under the tape. I'm sure she is calling me every name except a child of God. Hell I'll shoot her if she calls me that. My name is Ms. Malakai.

I rip the tape and she screams, "You fucking bitch."

"Open your fucking mouth; I need to check to see if you sucked his dick."

"You are crazy as those letters you mailed."

"You haven't seen crazy yet. I'm not going to ask you again. Have you sucked his dick in the office?"

"You dress like a slutty assistance. I know you got the job with your mouth. If I have to cut out your tongue and scrape his semen, I will."

"Benito put some fresh tape around this hoe. I believe the man of the hour is entering."

"How do you know? I haven't heard anything."

"When you love a man deeply, you know the sound of his brakes screeching when he's pissed."

"Hurry up before he runs in here and kill us both."

I hid behind the bar and wait on my Prince Charming. A tear drops wishing my sister could be here to embrace this with me. I wipe my lashes and return to my combat position.

He rushes in and shouts, "Monique who the hell parked in my space?"

Damn his voice makes my pussy wet; now is not the time.

"Man you have a few seconds to release her and get the fuck out my club."

Benito shouts, "Fuck you and your club. I'll let this bitch go when you leave with Necole."

I open my bags, jump from the bar with my tranquilizer gun and screams, "Surprise, I'm here."

He rolls his eyes and remarks, "You have a death wish."

"You gave that promise to Nikki not me. Don't worry, she won't interfere with us again. I killed her last week."

Benito interrupts and yells, "What the fuck you mean you killed her. What the fuck is going on Necole?"

Malakai laughs and say, "You are a pawn in her world, this split personality bitch is crazy and you have been eating out of her hands."

I blow him a kiss and answer, "I'm crazy in love for you boo."

He notices the blood pouring from Monique's legs and asks, "Are you okay?"

She shakes her head verifying she is.

"Benito rip the tape from that bitch mouth again."

"I'm not doing shit until you tell me the truth."

"Okay since your balls are in knots. Yes, I killed my sister but you buried Charles and agreed to be a part of this. We have recorded your role since the beginning. If something happens to me, a special friend will look for you. Now rip the damn tape."

The second scream out of Monique mouth was sexier than the first.

"Malakai?"

"What the fuck you want?"

"Dick and kids but it will come later."

He shakes his head in disgust not knowing it's turning me on. I count my darts and line them on the bar.

"Malakai I need to know. Have you fucked Monique and if you answer wrong, Benito will put a bullet in her head?"

He shouts, "I never touched her. Let her go!"

"Have you thought about it?"

"I'm not answering shit."

Loading my first tranquilizer dart, "Malakai I believe you haven't fucked her but you thought about it."

"You love teasing women, getting pussy wet at shows and throwing them back in the crowd like trash. I promise I'm the last bitch fed to the wolves."

"Necole I'm tired of these games. You aren't going to kill me so this is how it will happen. I'm going to put a bullet through Benito, free Monique then strangle your ass until your eyes pop out."

Benito places the gun against Monique's head and ready to fire at the sound of my voice.

"Malakai you don't have any authority right now. If you value her life, you better do as I say. Toss your gun and hold your hands up."

He kicks it across the floor, grabs his dick and say, "You want me to hold this up too."

"You are hilarious baby. Maybe you should become a poetic comedian."

"I'm not your damn baby. Do whatever so she can receive medical attention."

"That's your problem, always worrying about other hoes. Don't panic I won't let your precious assistance bleed out. I love her work ethics; she can work with me as her new boss."

"Monique I'm sorry I got you into this. I promise everything will be ok."

Okay, now I'm upset. I aim and release the trigger. The dart sails through the air striking him in the chest. His eyes float to it, grips around the dart and yanks it out.

"Bitch you'll need more than this to stop me from killing you."

I load the second one and fire in his direction striking his leg.

"Malakai I'm not going to kill you. I can't trust you to behave so these darts are filled with Valium. It won't be long before it's nighty-night for you."

I shoot two more and he drops to one knee.

"Benito! Catch and knock him the fuck out. Don't hurt him."

He flips and busts a champagne bottle over his head. He falls flat on the ground barely moving.

Benito asks, "What's next?"

"Put his ass in the car. You'll get your money and we never have to see each other again."

"I don't want to see you either especially since you played me from day one. I thought you were identical twins."

"Benito shut the hell up talking shit. If you want to know the truth, Nikki considered you a great face fuck. If you don't believe she's dead, maybe you will believe this. She ran away with a white man and wasn't coming back. Matter of fact she met him the same night at the restaurant."

He drops his head in shame and not sure why he's upset. He fucked two women in one night, that's equivalent to an *Oscar*'s award for men.

He lifts Malakai and drags him out the door.

I grab my items, scroll to Monique and remind her, "We are alone. I don't like you but your work ethic is flawless. Don't go to the police. I can't live without him so if anyone looks for him; they will discover a *Romeo and Juliet* scene."

She lifts her head with a grim expression and say, "Asperilla won't go for this. She will come for him."

I jab my finger in the bullet hole and snatch it out, "She's dead. I made sure of it before I came. The police found her face splattered on the windshield. Your phone will be by the door. You can limp or crawl to call 911."

"Necole you are lucky you have a gun."

"You are right, I am."

I discharge a bullet in her other thigh and kick her in the face, "Bitch you are under new management. You will respect me."

I meet Benito outside and he confirms, "Malakai is unconscious."

I reach inside my bag, toss the money and disclose, "Thanks for everything. Enjoy your new life."

He runs from the club to the car parked down the street.

As for me I sit in my seat, inhaling the scent of Malakai as my new car smell. Umm, I can drink this man blood.

I start the car and flip the rearview mirror. My lips trembles when I see Nikki in the backseat. I turn my head to make sure she wasn't there. I gasp for air, thinking she is plotting revenge. Nah she can't come back from the dead or could she?

I shake my head and shout, "No No No! You aren't going to ruin this. I worked to damn hard. Get out of my head."

I rub my eyes for a clearer visual and no one is there.

I slither my hands between Malakai thighs and caress his dick. Don't worry baby, not even a ghost will stop us from being together.

Chapter 37

Asperilla

The person you're trying to reach is unavailable. If you need further assistance, enter pound now. Thank you and goodbye.

Isabella where are you? You better not be somewhere fucking off. I knew I should have rescheduled it for another time.

I let out a heavy sigh. Let me call the event coordinator. "Good Afternoon my name is Asperilla Valdez. I'm scheduled for a conference call today. I sent my cousin Isabella down with the proposal."

"Please hold."

"Yes we had you down for noon but your party was a no-show. Is there anything else I can assist you with?"

"No ma'am. Thank you."

My cousin knows how important this is. I have a gut feeling something is wrong.

I toss the phone on the bed. Fuck, it's time to investigate. Luckily, I'm dressed but my wardrobe wouldn't be complete without a lace garter holster with my *P380*. I readjust my sundress, head downstairs, approach the door and the buzzer at the gate alarms. I take a sneak peek at the camera and Officer Pernell flashes his badge.

What the hell does he want? I haven't beaten a bitch ass since that white chick.

I press the button and open the front door to meet them. They need to hurry up because I have to find my cousin.

"Asperilla we are truly sorry to bother you at this time. We have a couple of questions for you."

I roll my eyes, switch my purse to my other hand and say, "Please make it fast."

"Do own a blue 2015 *Jaguar XJ* with the license plate X69QFA?"

"Yes the same one you gave a ticket in last month. Where are you going with this?"

"There was an accident earlier on the scanner with a car that fits your description. I wasn't at the scene but a fellow officer recognized the plate. I rushed to check on you since I was in the neighborhood. I tried calling Malakai but no answer."

Damn what the fuck is he's doing and why he can't answer his phone? He better not be slanging dick like the old days or I'm going to-

"Asperilla, this is important, are you listening to me?"

"Yea sure, go ahead. A car similar was in an accident." Shit. Isabella. Where is the car now? Is everyone okay?"

"Is seemed to be a hit and run. There were bullet casings at the scene as well."

"Bullets, what the fuck?"

"I'm not sure of all the details but the driver was taken to *Tampa General*."

"Officer Pernell try to contact Malakai again; I have to go."

I run to the garage, unlock the *Hummer* and speed down the street. I will find who's responsible.

I'll kill over my girls but when you fuck with my family, it's another ballgame. I will mutilate, dissect and resurrect to kill them again.

I slap my hands across the steering wheel. Dammit, I should have gone to the meeting.

The speedometer floats to 100 as I weave through traffic. Blowing my horn, yelling out my window and flipping my finger.

I arrive at the main entrance, throw cash at the valet attendant and say, "Don't scratch my shit."

Dashing through the door in my heels; the elevator is closes and I scream, "Hold the door."

A snobbish woman turns her nose up and ignores my request. She let it close before I arrive. I bolt through the stairwell pissed off. I beat the elevator to the main formation table. Huffing a little, I ask the clerk, "Please tell me what floor Isabella Valdez is on."

She types a few keys and answers, "She's in surgery right now. Are you an immediate family member?"

Remember Asperilla, she is only doing her job.

I lower my tone and reply, "Yes I am. Can I please go up?"

The nurse's aide gives the room number. Turning into the woman that wouldn't leave the door open. I slap her face and she spins into the arms of the next person.

"Next time, hold the door, you selfish bitch."

I make it to the desk and the nurse is on the details.

She suggests, "Sit in the waiting room and I'll notify the doctor to speak with you."

Tears are in people's eyes but mine shows pure hate.

I reach inside my purse to check my phone. No missed call from my jackass fiancé. I dial his number and it goes straight to voicemail.

"*I'm not sure where you are or why you aren't answering your phone. I'm at Tampa General waiting to see Isabella. She was in a hit and run. Whatever you are doing. Stop and get your ass here.*"

After a thirty-minute wait, the doctor announces, "Ms. Asperilla Valdez."

I jump from my seat and ask, "How's she doing?"

"Her injuries are not critical but she needs time to heal. God was in the car because the first bullet went through the driver's window and out the passenger. I believe it caused her to lose control of the vehicle. The second bullet penetrated her shoulder but the airbag created damage also. Her face is bruised, neck and back pain but no internal bleeding. We are conducting a second CT scan to make sure she doesn't have any brain hemorrhaging. Her X-rays are negative for broken bones but she is conscious."

"Can I see her?"

"Yes but give us a second to leave the room and you can check on her."

Thank you Jesus for sparing my cousin. I know you are shaking your head in heaven at my thoughts. Yes, I'm praising you and will repent for killing the person that did this. I try to change but people prefer to see the monster in me.

I straggle to Isabella room, unsure of the image I will encounter. Her eyes are closed and face looks like she was stomped in a gang fight. Black eyes, busted lips and an IV running through her arm.

My thought is Aunt Sofia is going to kill me for letting this to happen to her.

I stroke my fingers through her hair whispering, "Everything will be okay. I'll find out who did this."

She opens her eyes and softly speaks, "Hey cousin."

"Don't say a word, save your strength."

"I'm sorry I didn't deliver your proposal."

"No worries, the only thing on my mind is a funeral. Go ahead and rest. I'm happy that you are alive."

"Your car is totaled."

"Yes, more than a scratch."

She attempts to laugh but feels the pain from the injury.

"The police will ask questions once you are feeling better. Remember to tell them you don't know shit."

"Hell I don't know shit, it happened so fast."

"Great answer, now go to sleep. I'll be sitting her all night."

This is not the image I want to see. I pull out my phone to call Malakai and Monique name flashes across the screen.

"Hello?"

"Oh my God, you are alive."

"What the fuck you talking about Monique? Where's Malakai?"

"I can't tell you over the phone but I'm in the hospital."

"Which one?"

"*Tampa General*. I'm in room 3606, please come."

I shake my head from the disturbing news, disconnect the call and peep at Isabella.

She falls asleep quicker than I thought.

I sneak to Monique's room to what she has to say.

The elevator door opens and I walk to her room, "I'm here, what's going on?"

She lays in the bed with her laptop working on a spreadsheet of the club revenues.

"Monique you're a trooper. Put that damn shit away before I toss it out the window."

"What the hell are you doing here?"

"I thought you were dead at least that's what the crazed stalker told me."

I slam my fist against the wall. I knew this wasn't a coincidence. She shot at my cousin and ran her off the road. "What the hell did she do to you?"

She flips the covers revealing her bandaged thighs, "Yes. This is the work of your man's psychotic bitch."

"I thought Malakai took care of her. Where the fuck is that nigga?"

"She drugged and kidnapped him."

"What the fuck? I told him to put a bullet in her and be done with it. Poetry is going to be the death of him. He didn't want to kill her because she's a fan but my cousin is upstairs because of his hesitations. If Isabella wasn't involved, she could keep him."

"Asperilla, you are joking right?"

"Hell no. Fuck him. He knows how I am about my family. She probably strapped him to a bed and forcing him to recite love poems. How did he get drugged?"

"This hoe had a tranquilizer gun. The kind used for cattle. I didn't think you could use it on humans."

A twisted smile appears and Monique asks, "What are you thinking of?"

"I'm glowing; that is some shit I'll do. Enough of that, how did you get caught up?"

"I was on my way to the club when I was attacked by a guy and forced inside. He gagged and held me until Necole stormed through the door. There was no way I could have warned him about her hiding behind the bar. She shot me twice and said she's leaving me alive to manage the club."

"I'm sorry Monique. Now that you are ok I can get my jokes in."

I hike my skirt displaying my garter holster. "You need to get you one of these, bang!" I shout.

"What did the police say?"

"I didn't call them. I called security, faked like I was in a drive by and was admitted. They are at the club cleaning up as we speak.

"When did they say you can leave?"

"I will be here for a minute; you don't have to worry about the club. I have taken care of everything and can manage it from here."

"You are lying in the bed with bullet holes and the only thing you can think about is the venue. Fuck that! You should have shut it down for a couple of days. They would be alright to miss a weekend."

"Malakai would kill us."

"Fuck him too. He is busy with his groupie."

"Do you remember what the guy looked like?"

"Yes he's an Italian named Benito."

"Thanks I'll go by the club and pull surveillance. I'm sure I can get a great face recognition."

"Asperilla please be careful, especially since you are pregnant."

I rub my stomach, "We will be okay. She needs her daddy."

"Is it a girl?"

"Hell I don't know. I'm going to keep saying a girl. I don't have time for a little boy running around smelling his dick like his stinking ass Papi. Today could have been worse. The bitch is crazy but I'm going to make sure she knows who's crazier. I will call one of the girls to sit with you and don't get on that laptop today."

"I'll do my best but I can't make any promises. I understand why Malakai loves you running the spot."

"I'll see you tomorrow. I have to check on Isabella."

"Asperilla?"

"Yes?"

"I'm sorry all of this happened before your wedding."

"Yeah all types of shit occur when you are *Married to the Pen*."

Chapter 38

Malakai

I blink my eyes a couple times to focus on my surrounding. The wilderness scent floats by my nose and from the window I see a lake. I attempt to move my arms and legs but it is useless. I turn my head to see what's holding me.

Aww Shit, this bitch chained me to the wall with a *CB-6000* locked to my dick.

"Good morning sleepyhead. Did you have a lovely dream about me?"

I rattle the chains and answer, "I had dreams of flushing your head down the toilet."

She kisses my cheek and asks, "You are such a kidder, and that's why I love you. Do you love my outfit?"

The man in me wants to say hell naw but the whore peeps the French maid lingerie costume when she entered the room. The mesh halter apron, sexy G-string, wrist cuffs, and headband are seductive.

She sits the tray of food and say, "I'll feed you for strength to get me pregnant. I'm ovulating this week and if it's a girl we will name her after my deceased sister Necolette."

"Unchain me and this chastity belt from my dick."

"Why? It looks beautiful wrapped around your thick, muscular meat piece. I asked more than once if you wanted to wear it."

"How could I respond when I was drugged and unconscious?"

She giggles, places her hand over her mouth and say, "Oops my bad. I don't give a fuck what you say Malakai. You're always saying how your dick is a beast and the 10th wonder of the world. Consider me your zookeeper and can brag to the world that I captured the savage monster."

Listen folks, here is the great Malaki. No worries ladies his dick is harmless, tamed and can't escape from the CB-6000 made of medical grade polycarbonate material. Notice the curved cage with versatile ring system. It's perfect to restrain a well-endowed gentleman. This cage is design for long term wear and used with numbered plastic locks allowing the wearer to pass through metal detectors without setting off alarms.

"How many ladies have you fucked?"

"That's a dumb ass question. How many men have your crazy ass fucked?"

"Baby please don't make me upset, you wouldn't like me when I'm angry. I am going to ask you again and will say it slowly. Howwwww Mannny Ladieeees Haveeeee Youuuu Fuckkkkk?"

"I didn't fuck you or your loony ass sister."

"Sigh, baby you are as hardheaded as your dick. It's ok, I'll teach you some respect. Men always thinking they can disrespect a woman and get away with it. Not today."

She walks to the table and retrieves a sharp object. She pokes a pair of 4 ½ inch vise in my nose.

"Are you sure you don't want to answer my questions?"

I roll my eyes and say, "I refuse to answer dumb shit."

"Have it your way Mr. *Burger King.*"

She opens the vise grip, clamp my nipples and squeeze until blood leaks down my pecs.

"Got damn that feels good. Do the next one baby, I love that freaky shit."

She releases and says, "I knew we were meant to be. You are kinky like me. You need to answer my questions."

"Okay Necole, should I start by race and age? Do threesome counts as twos?"

She slaps my face similar to the wind blowing through the trees. She has my full attention. I hate when a woman touches my face.

I shake the chain and say, "Bitch once I'm free, your ass is mine."

"Whatever boy, stop calling me names. You didn't have the heart to kill my sister so I know you not going to do anything to me. I know you are hungry, answer the questions and maybe I'll take the chastity belt off."

"Females always want to know answers I don't have. I was a fucking whore; I averaged women like NBA points."

She sits in the chair, crosses her legs and say, "Do tell Mr. Stroker. Enlighten me on how many ladies you misused and left emotionally dead."

I blurt out, "200."

"That's all?"

"You didn't give me the chance to finish. I blazed that number last year before I went into retirement. If I had to give you a roundabout figure. Umm, maybe 2,500 women in my lifetime."

"Impressive numbers. I'm shock you don't have a lot of kids running around the country. You are a bad boy Malakai and deserves to be punished."

"You ought to thank me for saving you from the wrath of females. Now my next question is why are fans off limits?"

"I can answer that with ease. I never wanted to fuck up my art. Poets are ruining the game by fucking fans and groupies. There are some crazy people out there. No disrespect to you," I chuckle.

She reverses her legs, "Oh I'm not offended. I know you are talking about them."

What the hell is wrong with her?

"When a woman falls in love with your work, you develop a sacred bond; they become a part of your world. You rejoice when they smile, blessed when they take pictures with your work and transform them from fan to family. You develop deep, passionate eternal love and don't want to mess it up over a one-night stand."

"Eww that means you will be my cousin and Necole don't do incest."

"Yeah we are related and you should let me go."

"Aww fuck, I can make an exception for you. Consider me the horny auntie and you are the young nephew. We can play in a minute."

I'm never getting out of here, I might as well be friendly since I'm hungry at least her idiotic ass can cook.

"What do you have for breakfast over there?"

She lifts the cover, squat over the food and say, "Green eggs and pussy. I bet you didn't know I was sexy and funny; see all the fun you've been missing. I will clean you up first before you eat."

She sits a pan of steamy and soapy water between my legs. Bends over and squeezes the wash cloth, showing glimpses of her ass cheeks with a tattoo of a man's face. My eyes trail her back and a scorpion tattoo with my name.

"Nice ink work."

"I'm glad you noticed; my sister designed it."

"Whose face is on your ass?"

"Baby the medicine has you delirious, I only have one tattoo."

I lean my head against the wall wishing I had blown her brains out.

She wipes my chest with a damp wash cloth, opens her mouth and sucks the blood from my nipples. Her lips create a tantalizing shooting pleasure to my toes. I won't admit the joy to her of how good her mouth feels.

I'm sending secret codes to my dick not to get aroused around this freak. Men can say what they wouldn't do in certain situations but rehab didn't prepare me for this. If I escape without fucking her, I know I will pass. I have to resist because of Asperilla and the baby. It's easier to turn a woman down when you aren't alone to watch pussy lips and titties.

She removes her lips, licks the tip and say, "All clean. Let's eat before the food gets cold."

She twists her ass back to the food, return with a plate of grilled chicken and scrambled eggs with cheese.

"I know this is one of your favorite entrees. I followed your posts on *Instagram* and knew I could top any restaurant you have dined. I practiced it once a week until perfection.

She lifts the food to my mouth and say, "Taste it."

I chew the first bite. The chicken is grilled with special seasoning and the eggs are delicious. Curiosity strikes my mind and I need to know.

"How did you get the recipe?"

"Easy. I kidnapped the chef. No, I didn't kill him."

"Is Monique okay?"

"I know your mother taught you not to talk with your mouth full."

"But I'm not eating anything."

"Your mouth is full of shit. Don't ask me about another bitch when I'm serving you. Now finish eating and you can assist me with my masturbation exercises."

I rattle the chain and thrust my chastity belt upward and say, "What do you expect me to do tied up."

"My dear Malakai, you have a sweet mouth. I'm sure you can use it for something incredible."

She takes the empty plate, undress and stares in my face, "You will spit poetry until I cum on your toes and if it's real nasty, it won't take long."

"And if I refuse."

She tiptoe and tug on my earlobe with her teeth and say, "I'll use the vise grip to snatch your balls; now spit something."

I've memorized over 100 poems and I can't remember shit. She slitters her tongue down my thighs and bite my calf muscles. She pinches her nipples, plunges her fingers in her clit and say, "I'll unlock the belt if you do something erotic and slutty."

She rises and grabs the key from the table and releases my dick; pouncing over her nose like a runaway slave seeking freedom.

"Oh baby I think it loves me. Cum to Mama."

She sinks her nails in my flesh, stretches her tongue out like a frog dabbing it against my head and slurping on the side wiggling my balls.

"Baby I waited so long to give my Slobberknocker. Don't make me regret taking the belt off. Fuck me with your words."

This is the moment of survival and poetry has always been my life line. I see her neck muscle swelling as she inhales my dick down her throat. She finger fucks her slit and juices run down her arms.

"Aww Fuck."

My dick mutates to a wilder beast and her throat game inspires a poem like never before.

> *Have you ever been to a baby shower where a woman*
> *can drain you of your power?*
> *I am talking about standing buck naked while a woman*
> *is on her knees.*
> *Her head game is so good that every time she pulls*
> *your skin, your butt cheek automatically squeezes.*
> *I am looking at her lips and they are enticing.*
> *She has a mouthpiece that is perfect for slicing and*
> *dicing.*
> *I am talking about how she can deep throat and then*
> *scrap with her teeth. Damn that will drive any man crazy.*
> *She moans as she slurps then stops and whispers*
> *I want you to impregnate my throat with your delicious*
> *coat of cream and juice.*
> *If my dick was made of words, then her mouth is a*
> *home for verbal abuse.*
> *She said her mouth has gravity like the black hole.*

Equip to swallow any pole.
This I had to see. Tonight her mouth and I are going
half on a baby.
I twist my fingers in her hair as she begins to press
down on my head.
She said she like to leave her eyes wide open so she can
watch my emotions.
Baby the only thing you will see is sweat because
I am about to pump your tonsils with slow locomotion.
I take my time grinding against her tongue.
She begins to slurp and spit.
You know a Freak like that nasty shit.
She deep throats me then back with a winding tongue.
I promise if she did that one more time,
I probably would have been done.
Her moans become louder and grunts become harder.
I begin to thrust a little deeper.
I am sucking my stomach in like I am shooting
torpedoes with every stroke.
She laughs and say is that all you got.
Necole I am about to leave cum stains on the inside of
your brain.
I love a woman that talk shit and this is the only time
I will call a woman a Bitch but I'll call you anything
when your lips are press between my dick.
I pop my ass like I'm doing Hip Hop abs, dancing in
her mouth.
She's from Cali but I'm Alabama South.
She grabs my booty cheeks and pulls me in. I grab her
shoulders so we can be on one accord.

I close my eyes because I 'm about to pump out her insides.
We are slutty raw at this moment, sweat dripping. I'm yelling. You want these seeds;
Muthafucka do you want these seeds?
I can't hear you with your mouthful.
She mumbles UMM HMM,
I place one leg on her shoulder and pump everything into her mouth, juices and saliva are bouncing back on my stomach.
Oh I love this now.
I must admit she's a trooper and she is taking it hard and strong.
She twists my dick with her hands while she slurps.
Her nose is rubbing against my pelvic.
I am on the back of my heels beating her face.
Impact after Impact.
Moaning don't stop, Dammit, don't stop.
She's such a good woman because she obeys as I slay her mouth like a dragon.
Off with her head.
I can feel my nut rising from my gut.
I can feel the tension in my butt.
Necole I am about to cum and she moans and moans.
I grab the back of her head so I can have a direct aim.
I am about to strike gold and oil in her well.
I shoot and the first load knocks her face back but she swallows and stays on the attack.
The second load came with a harder force. I do believe her mouth has its own 18th hole golf course.
She drains every drop and every sip.

The rest she spreads on her lips like gloss.
She said it taste like secret sauce.
If her mouth ran for President, I'll cast my vote but
tonight I am glad I was invited to a
Baby Shower in her Throat.

Tears roll after finishing my last line. I worked my ass off being faithful and this bitch is drinking my nut like a shake.

She wipes her mouth and says, "Damn, got damn, your seeds have to be produced in the Garden of Eden, best nut I have guzzled."

She wipes my face and boasts, "Baby this is the first time I made a man cry."

My thoughts float, *"Bitch I'm not crying over you. I know Asperilla is going to kill us both."*

Chapter 39

Asperilla

"Cherry I'm pulling in the driveway; wake Jaz up. I throw the car in park, run to the door and scream, "Hurry the hell up."

My hair in the infamous bun with hidden razor blades, army fatigues and steel toe boots.

Cherry swings the door and asks, "Where are you going Rambo?"

"Afghan, Vietnam and down the street to Iraq in a few. Shut the hell up and sit your ass down. Where the fuck is Jaz?"

"She had a long night with one of her Johns; she will be down in a minute. What is the emergency this morning?"

"I need you all to take time off, go to the hospital and watch over Monique and Isabella."

"Oh my God!" She screams, "What happened?"

"I never told ya'll about Malakai's groupie but she snapped yesterday. She ran Isabella off the road, shot Monique in the club and kidnapped my man. I checked the footage from the club and I'm on my way to find this guy named Benito. I believe he has information where she has taken him."

"You should be celebrating and planning your wedding, do you want us to handle this?"

"This is personal besides she is a smart piece of shit. The hoe tricked me into buying her a wedding dress."

I catch Jaz stepping down from the corner of my eye, twisting her hair and asking, "What's the emergency?"

"Cherry knows the game plan. They are at *Tampa General*; I need both of you there within an hour. Keep your phones on. If you haven't heard from me in 48 hours, call Kryptonite and tell him to spray the city down. I would love to stay and chat but time is wasting. Go ahead and plan my bachelorette party while ya'll are bored. After this adventure, I need to see plenty of dicks, naked bartenders and the finest bi-sexual ladies in the city."

"Straps and hard ons for everyone. We will give you a party filled with everlasting memories."

"Great! I can't wait but I have to save my man first."

I give them a hug and return to my car. After hacking one of Malakai's emails, discovering her information from Undercover Brothers; this bitch will pay dearly."

I need some crunk killing music. I build my playlist on *Pandora*. Oh yeah, I found the best song *"What you Gon to do* by *Lil John.* This is a slaughter's anthem. I am bobbing my head, beating the steering wheel and throwing my hands out the window. I should discharge a few rounds down the causeway but I can't afford going to jail before I deliver the devil's daughter.

I arrive at her apartment, pop my trunk and see my weapon of choice. I know she is not there but I'm praying Benito is around. I like medieval weapons and my 36-inch spiked mace ball will do the trick. It has twenty-one spikes, stainless steel and all black. I lick the tip of the spike hoping to find a head to smash.

Whistling my theme song as I approach the door. I attempt to pick her lock as my hand grazes the knob and it slides open.

I shrug my shoulders and say, "Guess she was in a hurry to leave."

I scan the room assuring the coast is clear. I dash in and ransack the bedrooms. I am looking for one thing and getting the hell out. After checking the closets, I find it lying on her bed.

Yes! The stupid hoe left it. I'll make sure it's return to her.

I stop in my tracks after hearing a phone ring as I pass the kitchen. Searching through papers and find it in the utensil drawer.

My luck couldn't have been better.

"Hello? Who's this?"

I didn't answer. I want to hear him breathe.

"Quit playing on the phone before I beat your ass. You cheated me out a few thousands and I want the rest."

"How much I owe you?"

"Who's this? What are you doing with Necole's phone?"

"Come and find out?"

"I haven't got time for this bullshit."

"It's cool; I'm coming to find you anyway. See you later."

"Bitch come on over. I'm ready for fresh lips around my dick."

"I'm playing with my pussy now, tell me more."

"I'll fuck your throat raw and cum on your face."

"My mouth waters for your love. Can we meet in an hour?"

"Damn right and be ready to have your throat busted. When I'm done I'm splitting yours for talking shit."

"I can't wait. Give me the address and I'm there."

"I'm in *South Tampa*, 2514 W Jetton Avenue."

He hangs up the phone and I love a man to talk shit. Men are the stupidest muthafuckas in the world. Brute force will never defeat wet pussy.

I gather what I came for and prance to my car to meet his punk ass.

The drive is peaceful to a suburban neighborhood. I circle the block and notice a young man on the porch; I'm not sure how many are in the house. I park a few blocks and decide how to fit in. I check my back seat and all I have is workout clothes.

I arch my eyebrows and think, "This will do."

I slip into a pair of fitted print shorts and a halter top; it's great my stomach is flat. I lace my *New Balance*, step out the car and flash water on my face and chest. I perform a few stretches, grab my *Silver Haute Death Couture Fashion Knuckle*, place a few knives in my armband and jog down the block. Fuck a sports bra; I'm honor to have titties to bounce in the wind. I know my ass giggles with every stride. I pass a few new mothers along the way pushing strollers and this time next year I'll be doing the same.

Once I reach the 24th block, I sprint faster, approach 25th and come across *Jetton Ave*. I run pass his house, trip on purpose and land on the payment.

He rushes off the porch and asks, "Are you okay?"

I size him up to make sure he's not packing. He is busy looking at my ass, he doesn't notice the knuckles.

"Do you have any bottled water inside?"

"Follow me; we have some *Dasani*."

Inviting me is similar to vampires entering your home and I'm out for blood. He's a cute young man, wrong place at the wrong time though.

I follow him to the kitchen and he gives me a water out the refrigerator.

I run the bottle down my chest and asks, "Is anyone else here with you?"

"Yes, he ran upstairs after bragging about a sexy female coming over. Are you her?"

"Am I sexy enough to be her?"

"You are fine as hell but honestly if you are her, please go home. I think he wants to do something terrible. He's my partner but I don't get down with his wicked shit. He has acted strangely since he quit his job at the restaurant and dating some chick name Necole or Nikki."

He tells everything and doesn't know anything about me. This is why you have to run with closed mouth people. Maybe Benito screwed him out some pussy or money.

I sip my water and say, "You should leave. I'm here on business and you don't need to be involved."

"You bitches are all the same. A man tries to warn you about danger but you insist on doing it your way. Don't be surprised when your family sees your pretty face on *Bay News 9.*"

I shake my head, ball my fist and uppercut him. I ram my knees in his face; blood spews out his nose and mouth. Once he hit the floor, I snatch my blades out my armband, place my hand over his mouth and slice his throat. Sooner or later someone will do him in; he smells like a snitch. The world can thank me later.

I pick up his phone, creep upstairs and hear Benito singing in the shower.

I wait patiently for the water to stop. I text him saying, *"Your bitch is downstairs. I left her in the house for you."*

I hear the message and he opens the door running naked towards the staircase. I sneak behind him, kick him down and watch his head tumble over the steps. Stalking closer and he lies on the ground holding his ankle.

I grip the knuckles tighter and lunge into his throat. His breath becomes short and he wheezes from the impact. I jump in the air, landing my foot on his twisted ankle and pound the brass knuckles repeatedly over his bone.

"Aww shit I think you cracked my ankle."

"Shut the hell up."

"Where the fuck is Necole?"

He swings at me and misses by a mile.

"Damn you still trying to fight, I promise you won't get a chance to hit a woman again."

I reach in my hair for my blade. I ferociously slice through his skin, shredding his face and chest.

He screams and shouts, "Okay, I'll tell you."

"I don't have all day to fuck with you. I knew you were a bitch boy. What killer takes a shower before a woman comes? You are fucking with the wrong bitch. I'm going to ask you again, where did she take Malakai?"

"Asperilla?"

I punch him in the nose, "Yea muthafucka it's me. You two have fucked up my wedding plans and someone has to pay."

"She took him to *Paradise Lakes* the Nudist Resort. I think she has him at the lake house."

I punt my foot deep in his nuts, praying they cough out his mouth.

I sit on the sofa thinking how to kill this idiot. In the meantime, I place a call to my favorite reptile shop.

"Hank, this is Asperilla. Do you have two dozen Bens I can purchase? Wonderful, I'll be there today to pick them up."

"Well Benito it looks like my time is up and so is yours."

"What are you talking about? I didn't do anything."

Walking towards the kitchen, he grabs my ankle and I shake him loose. "Get the hell off of me."

I search the drawers for the biggest knife. My eyes sparkle when I see something better. His friend did say he worked in a restaurant and here's a meat cleaver. My pussy lips quiver from the impulse.

I hide it behind my back and approach him. One more question, you like to beat defenseless women. Is that true?" "Fuck it! You will lie anyway."

I swing the cleaver, split the middle of his face before he responds. Blood gushes from the head to his mouth.

"You won't hit another woman again," I state.

I pull the cleaver out revealing a crater in the middle of his face. I whistle my *Lil John* song and grip his dick.

"Damn Benito, you have a good piece of meat."

I flap it over his stomach and chop it like a hotdog on a meat board.

I wash my hands, wipe my mess and jog to my car. Press play on the playlist and find another murderous song to bob my head to leave.

Chapter 40

Asperilla

I recon the house and Malakai is alive. I'm pissed seeing her licking his nuts like a dog in heat. I can easily shoot her ass through the window but it's too easy. She needs to suffer for trying to kill my cousin.

Lugging this bag through the woods is exhausting; I'll be damn if I make more than one trip.

Once I reach my destination, I snatch my fiberglass shovel and dig her final resting place. I line it up, stomp the first drive with my foot and wedge it back. The more I reminisce on the day I bought her a wedding dress motivates me to dig harder. This bitch played on my kindness; something I don't display often.

Slamming my foot in the shovel, "You fucked up my plans."

A thick pile of dirt comes up when I snap the shovel back and toss it to the side. Within 45 minutes I am finished. I toss the shovel and climb out.

Shit. I need a break.

I sit in my quad chair, twist the cap off and drink water nonstop to quench my thirst. It's dark as hell out here; quiet except for the hooting owl in the tree.

Sigh. I guess it's time to save Malakai from this freaky hoe. Instead of retiring from selling pussy, his dumbass should give up poetry. This shit makes no sense to go through because of a psychotic fan. Least with the first lady we had a reason for someone to come after us.

I jump from my seat gathering my knives and guns, kill the beam from the portable light and follow the trail to the lake house.

I didn't realize the walk is about a mile. Motivation have you doing the unexpected. I sneak on the deck towards the den window. I notice Necole in the kitchen cooking dinner and it smells wonderful. I know Malakai's greedy ass is benefiting from her food. I tiptoe to the window where he is and tap. I hit it a few times to gain his attention. He turns his head in my direction and smile.

He motions with his lips, "I love you."

I place two fingers on my lips and touch the window. From my view I see a gun and keys on the table. I have to get into the house without creating a loud scene. One wrong move and she will kill both of them.

I tap the glass again and clamp my fingers together alerting Malakai to start spitting poetry. This will entertain her until I break in.

I scurry to the window to check on Necole. She takes the tray and head towards the other room.

Bout damn time.

I insert the tension wrench, click the lock pick gun and within seconds I am in. It's a little louder when it's peaceful outside; I hope she didn't hear me.

I grip the doorknob and pray Malakai keeps her attention. The worst feeling is opening the door and a gun is poking your forehead.

I exhale. Here goes nothing.

The aroma from the kitchen simmers through the air as I tip down the hallway.

I check my watch and the distraction should be here any minute. I slide in the second bedroom and text my backup crew.

I wait quietly in the dark room with my pistol pointing at the entrance. The doorbell rings ten minutes later and I hear footsteps trampling. This was Jaz's idea and hopefully gives me enough time to unchain Malakai.

I overhear Jaz and Cherry acting drunk and looking for a party. Those two never had a problem walking naked so they blended in perfectly.

I rush to the room, kiss Malakai and ask, "Where's the key?"

"She snatched it when the doorbell rang."

"Fuck me."

I switch the gun off safety, aim toward the door and express, "So much for a sneak attack."

"You are going to get us both killed."

"Shut the hell up. This is your fault. We wouldn't be here if you would have done what you were supposed to."

The door opens, my finger on the trigger and Necole steps in with a gun to Jaz's neck.

"How the fuck you get hemmed up, where's Cherry?"

"She's quicker than I thought. She knocked her out with the pistol and snatched me in the house."

"Asperilla you are supposed to be dead, I watched the car slam in the wall."

I grip my pistol tighter, "Naw Bitch, that was my cousin and you will pay for putting her in the hospital."

She wraps her hands around Jaz's neck, poke the barrel against her head and say, "It's okay. I have enough bullets to finish the job."

"You can only get one off before I unload in your chest. The odds are against you Necole."

She pushes Jaz, causing me to stumble and giving her enough time to place the gun on Malakai. I regain my balance but it's too late, she has the upper hand.

"Drop your piece or I'll blow his brains all over this room and it will be your fault. Neither one of us will have him."

"Necole fuck these hoes! I will marry you and give everything."

I guess it's my time to play the supporting actress. I cry out, "Malakai what the hell are you doing?"

He ignores me and tells Necole, "We can have as many kids you want."

She presses the pistol against his head and says, "If you love me, prove it. I want you to kill that bitch and her friend."

"Release me and I'll do whatever you command."

"Tell that bitch to toss her gun."

"You heard her, you fucking spick, do what she asks."

I force tears down my eyes, "Malakai I can't believe you are disrespecting me in front of this groupie."

Deep in my mind I'm praying this shit works or we are going to die. I lift my shirt revealing to Jaz that I have another gun. I hope she has enough sense to pass it to me.

I slide my gun in her direction but she never takes her eyes off me. A million things are going through my head; why didn't I follow her to the door when the bell rung?

Love, fucking love, caused me to run to my man first instead of killing her crazy ass. If I get out of here, I 'll never make that mistake again.

Necole looks at her reflection and her face displays a sinister look. She winks at Malakai and say, "Open your mouth."

"Anything for you baby."

She shoves the pistol in his throat, "Muthafucka I owe you."

I am shocked and stunned at her sudden reaction.

I shout, "Don't kill him; shoot me, shoot me."

Jaz catches the hint and unhooks my gun from the holster.

"Shut up Bitch and my name is Nikki. Your man is going to die. He is the reason my sister tried to kill me. I lost my boyfriend over her obsession. I might not make it out of here alive but Corbin knows if something happens, who to look for."

This crazy woman has lost her mind. I slip my hand behind me and motion for Jaz to give me the gun.

"Say goodbye to your man."

Everything goes in slow motion.

She pauses, pulls the gun and screams, "No Nikki, you can't kill Malakai. I love him."

The confrontation between her personalities create a split second to rush her, knock the gun out and punch her in the face.

She exchanges blows and sneak an uppercut in my stomach.

Once she hit me, my adrenaline explodes as I give her a left hook and a super uppercut knocking her to the ground.

Jaz picks up the gun and fires a shot in the air, hitting the ceiling. I am in beat down mode and nothing can stop me from whooping her.

I stomp her face repeatedly with my steel toes, "Bitch how dare you hit me in the stomach. Don't you know I'm pregnant?"

The last kick to her head knocks her out.

I catch my breath and say, "Damn this bitch is a fighter."

I search her pocket for the keys, toss them to Jaz and say, "Go unchain Malakai."

He comes from the wall, gives me a hug and says, "I owe you my life."

I release myself and kick him in the nuts, "That's for letting that bitch suck your dick."

"Jaz, stop looking at my man's dick, find some clothes, and check on Cherry to make sure she's okay."

"Alright, what are you going to do with her?"

"She has a date with death once she gets to her new location."

Malakai finds his clothes and say, "It's good you are pregnant now because I believe you fucked up my shit."

He kisses my lips and says, "I fucked up huh."

I roll my eyes and answer, "Duh."

Jaz returns with Cherry who has a big lump on the side of her head.

"Damn Cherry, you are always getting your ass kicked. We need to sign you up for martial art classes."

"Ya'll grab the gun; Malakai, carry your bitch."

We leave the lake house and hike up the trail under the moonlight. I shine my flashlight towards the rechargeable portable lights.

"Jaz keep the beam focused here to give us extra lighting.

Malakai drops his groupie on the ground and ask, "Now what?"

"There's some cold water over there. Wake her ass up and see which personality we are dealing with."

He pours the water on her until she wakes up fighting the air demonstrating she's drowning. I give her a moment to gain her bearings.

"Malakai what are we doing here, I thought you love me?"

I look in her face and say, "Bitch the only person that loves you is the devil and he's waiting on you."

"No Malakai. You promised that you were going to kill Asperilla. I kept my sister from killing you. I hate your ass."

I clap my heels together, grab the bag with my cute rats and whisper, "Malakai, it's time we dispose of her once and for all."

"Jaz if she sneezes wrong, shoot that bitch in the head but first grab the wedding dress I bought. Yeah you little slut, I went to your house, picked it up, and had it dry cleaned for your ceremony."

"Malaki hold her down and Cherry will put it on."

After a little struggle, she is dressed and ready for the death dealer.

She realizes it's the end, sits calmly, lowers her head and speaks to herself, "Nikki, I'm sorry I didn't listen. You should have killed Malakai when you had the chance."

Nikki responds, "it's okay sis. Corbin will avenge us."

She claps her hands and chant the *Color Purple* sister song *"Me and you, us never part. Makidada. Me and you, us have one heart. Makidada. Ain't no ocean, ain't no sea. Makidada. Keep my sister away from me."*

I place raw meat with two rats in a bag and tie it around her head. It didn't take long for them to eat into her flesh. Her screams increase from the torture.

I grab the gun from Jaz and release a bullet in each thigh, "Bitch that's for Monique. I'm the only woman she works for."

I plant my steel toes in the middle of her face, knocking her into the grave. I stand over her and think about Isabella in the hospital. I squeeze the trigger three more times, lodging them in her chest.

I aim one last time, the muzzle flash, bullet rip through the bag and pierce her head. Her body lies motionless, no sound from her or Nikki.

The nightmare is over and everyone is speechless except Malakai; he rubs my shoulder and says, "It's done. Let's go home."

"Not quite yet, I paid good money at the reptile shop. I dash back and pour the rest of the rats in the grave. Everyone grab a shovel. I made a promise to bury her in the dress."

We dig through the dirt covering another chapter in our life. Grace saved us tonight and that's the perfect name for my daughter. Gracyanne Valdez.

ACKNOWLEDGEMENTS

Special Thanks to my top-notch supporters.
You are the wind beneath my wings.

Creolistic Ink Publishing,
Johnathan Royal & Books, Beauty and Stuff,
Msbehavin's Madness, Iris Perkins, Adrienne Miller,
Tamaka Wright, Endless Design Braiding, Jen Robinson,
Kim Pollard, Sheila LeBlanc, Tunisha Maffett, Rose Pearl,
Jureka Johnson, Dormeka Wells, Retta Elder,
Monica Filmore, Ashley James, Lyrically Divine,
Jakita White, Chanel Frazier, Samantha Adams,
Trina Chatman, Lauren Lo-Lo Morales, Gregory Jackson,
Valencia Pease, Andre & Toni Parker, Vette Arnold,
Carmen Brisker, Chalon James, David & Sherry Williams,
Stephanie Torres, LaCheryl Jones, Brandy Sobolik,
Monique Carlise, Sadrina Lemondrop Perez,
Angela Harris, Danny Piett, Vickey Williams,
Teresa Jones, Detra Simmons, Laura Georgia-Peach Allen,
Pam Vincent, Donya Lee, Shoutel Cockham,
Keisha Murray, Art-N-Soul, Caroline Frazier,
Iesha Bynum, Chastaty Ellerbee, Tiana Necole,
Theresa Turner & Robert Gibson,
Shalonda Porter, April Marizette, Dara MzPain Williams,
Alesia A. Barcus, Angel Ann, Shantel LadyRed Rembert,
Mya Franks, Charlotte Martin, Nikki Green,
CaNeshia McNeal, Cheryl Sweehoney, Candace Mumford,
Poets Flows to You
Author Adrina Smith & Authoress CoCo,

Author Laquita Cameron & Author Stephanie Reynolds,
Author Naomi Matthews & Author J. Asmara,
Author Mashawn Mickels & Author Suga Shak,
Author Vita Coop & Author Monique Nixon,
Author Marcina Tastysunshine Gilliam,
Author Fabulous Fe's Freaky & Author Telesa Stanford.

Thank you to all of my supporters for the constant calls,
emails, videos and social media posts. My dreams are
manifested with your love and God's gift. Thanks for being
loyal, patience and supportive.

Flenardo Speaks

I am an ordinary man who decided to manifest my dreams into reality with a creative stroke of imaginative superpowers. My passion to do the unthinkable is the adrenaline rush towards the next adventures.

Thank you for reading *Married to the Pen*. The series wouldn't be complete without a Tantalizing Trilogy, coming in 2017.

To all my fans, I am giving you the pleasure of choosing the next book title. You can send your submissions to flenardo@gmail.com

If you haven't read the first book, *The Poetic Whore*; it can be found on Amazon and freknardo.com

You can find me on Instagram and FB under Flenardo Taylor.